THE LYNCHING TREE

by

Michael Stein

THE PERMANENT PRESS
SAG HARBOR, NEW YORK

Library of Congress Cataloging-in-Publication Data

Stein, Michael
    The Lynching Tree / by Michael Stein
        p. cm.
    ISBN 1-57962-070-1

    1. Police--New Jersey--Fiction. 2. Afro-American Police--
Fiction. 3. New Jersey--Fiction. 4. Lynching--Fiction.
    I. Title.
    PS3569.T3726 L96 2000
    813'.54--dc21   00-037356
                                                    CIP

THE PERMANENT PRESS
4170 Noyac Road
Sag Harbor, NY 11963

For my father

Acknowledgements

I am grateful to Dr. C. Bright, Deborah Norman and Jill Schlesinger for their advice on early drafts of this manuscript. Hester patiently read every version of this story and had me change a few thousand things. My work gets done because of her.

We are lived by powers we pretend to understand:
They arrange our lives; it is they who direct at the end
The enemy bullet, the sickness, or even our hand.

—W.H. Auden

THAT night, felt, seen, heard, not fully felt, not truly seen, scarcely heard, and still in me.

Awake, I try hard to recall—not that recollection is any use—what he wore, his face, what I saw or mis-saw when I looked at the night, when the boy stepped away from the wall. Perhaps the images I'm extracting from memory are the ones any man in my position would make up.

In the dull heat of this mechanical bed, a call button for my hand-shake, the walls as white as my mother's clothesline, there are moments when the shooting still seems imminent, and there are moments when that night vanishes. For as long as I live the images will be there in the first minute of my waking. I don't expect otherwise.

There are few hours when I can rest. I have always had the power to skip over whole days and nights as if they did not happen; this power is now a blessing.

I am here. Secrets have been locked in this room before, and I will leave secrets behind too. The land is full of young men like me, policemen wooed by fury, moving ahead with their eyes shut. But none, I think, as extreme as I.

What will I do next, where will I go?

Fucking nowhere.

The curtains are drawn, the windows tight, and I hear cars outside going too fast.

I am the one who wanted an answer to the lynching, and without an answer what is the point of my story? Only this: to explain is to be forgiven.

Butras was the one who wanted nothing. Outside, in the world, he proceeds with a certainty and purpose I envy.

My story is my story. It is history. It is not myth and hero. Does a black man telling this story mean anything to anyone?

•

MY first day at work when I saw Butras from across the back room of the police station, I saw teeth striking teeth. It was a strange thing to notice first, but it stuck in my mind.

Butras saw me and came over. When he squeezed my hand, he squeezed it hard and kept moving forward until we stood very close. By the time Butras stopped, it was as if we were in the center of a ring and we were scheduled to fight. I didn't realize then that he was someone from my past, although I figured there would probably be classmates from my high school on the force.

I could smell Butras' aftershave on his neck. It was a powerful, rum odor and Butras wore too much. Or perhaps it was the odor of panic in my own sweat.

In the glare of the squad room the other men, pacing back and forth in their slow black shoes, were drinking coffee from Styrofoam cups and smoking cigarettes. I studied the bookcase where trophies from teams the department sponsored were kept. The American flag sticker on the side of the bookcase read: "These colors don't run." I heard the noise—stories fighting other stories—and the forced click of the broken wall clock. If I shut my eyes and breathed in, it was the smoke and rattle of my freshman dorm. It was as if I were back at Rutgers.

I was told I would be sharing a car with Frank Butras from that Monday, the first of December to the end of the month. He would be my teacher. After the New Year I'd get my own car and I would work alone like the others.

Butras leaned toward me and whispered, "You're gonna get it now. Keep your head down." Then he turned toward the eight or ten guys seated near their tall blue lockers, some getting into their uniforms, others undressing, the end of one shift, the beginning of another.

"This is Donald Gambell, the newest product of the Academy," Butras introduced me.

"Should we tell him about you, Frank, or let him find out on his own?" The way they teased him I could tell he was well-liked.

Then I heard:

"We know who Gambell is."

"We've read about him in the paper. Pompan High. Recent college grad. Doing what he wants with his life."

Butras asked, "We all want to know: you satisfied with the spread you got in *The Record*?"

"Can't get a better story," I said.

I didn't tell the reporter who did the profile on me all the stupid things I'd done in Pompan; he was only interested in the positive, the new black officer who could "go where no man had gone before." I didn't tell him how I smashed my first motorcycle, driving late at night without a helmet, pulling into my driveway too fast, waking neighbors. I didn't tell him I'd been suspended from Pompan High for cutting classes sophomore year, and how my father had hit me for the last time the night he found out, how I caught his hand and warned him never to hit me again.

The reporter didn't seem to know I'd been written about in *The Record* years before.

"You'll have a good month working with the master," Tom Prescott said. Tom had black hair everywhere—inside his ears and nose, up his neck, thick on the tops of his hands. "Just remember that although he acts like an old man sometimes, he's only a few years older than you are. What are you Frank, 26? Oh, and Gambell, don't forget to cut us a break when you talk to the press again."

"Okay, that's enough," Butras said. Then he put his arm around my shoulder and guided me around the room as I shook hands with each, like it was a receiving line.

Around me, conversation shifted to other subjects:

"Where's Teddy today?"

"Hurt his hand."

"Oh, yeah?"

"Burned it."

"So you're in for him?"

"They couldn't do any better."

•

DURING the ride out on December 1st, Butras taught me how to handle calls and use the radio. He showed me around the district and taught me a few short-cuts. The town looked wealthier than I remembered it—more redwood decks and gas grills covered with black tarpaulins, more TV dishes on roofs and signs for house alarm systems. Butras seemed to know the history of every home and the people who lived in them. It was information I never had growing up there, near these very houses, or perhaps information I never paid attention to.

"That's the place where the Tinisher kid had the breakdown, went crazy, what have you. He wouldn't take his pills and it took seven of us to get him to the hospital.

"That's where Mr. Molotsky lives." He pointed to another house. "He's getting on in years and asked me to hold a key to his house. In case he needed someone to get in some time. Some one will ask you to do that when you've been around a while.

"Dennis Paul's house. Ten kids. Right now he's in the holding cell, daughter accused him of rape. I heard this banging when I came in the station the other day. Banging and banging in the back where the pens are, and no one is paying attention. We got five holding cells you know. And I go see what's happening and there's Dennis in a cell and I say, 'Dennis, what are you doing here?' and he says, 'They think I raped Carol, but I didn't, could you tell them I didn't Frank?' And I say, 'I'm not here to judge you Dennis. I have nothing against you.' And he wants to tell me the whole story, but I don't want to hear it. I mean I've known the guy my whole life. So I say, 'Is there anything I can do for you Dennis?' And he says, 'Yeah, they won't give me my contact lenses or my medicines.' I tell him, 'I can do that,' and that's why he's banging, because no one is treating him like a person just because his daughter accused him. But I don't know what happened, do I? And I'm not here to judge him because then anyone can go around judging me."

At 5:30 that afternoon, there was a demonstration at city hall about school budgets. We couldn't even get out of the station lot because of the traffic.

Butras said, "It's all right with me if everyone has a right to march. But don't go sitting down in the street and blocking traffic. If I'm hustling somewhere and you're in my way, I'm thinking: are you really that bad off that you're ruining things for me? And I have to believe, No Sir. Let's keep some perspective on things, fellas. You get yours and I get mine."

Butras leaned on the horn and wouldn't get off until some of demonstrators moved out of his way.

Butras said, "You know any of these people?"

"No one looks familiar," I answered.

He seemed disappointed. He was always asking me who I knew. For some reason, he figured if he didn't recognize someone, I would.

"I'm new here, you know," I said, trying to make a joke.

"No you're not," he said, irritated.

The late afternoon sun was almost gone. Butras continued to lean on his horn. A woman, about 30 years old in a red parka, gave us the finger.

Butras rolled down his window. What interested me was the tone of his voice.

"Is anything wrong?" he asked her.

She hesitated and glared.

"Well, is there?" he asked.

"You're making quite a noise out here," she said.

"I knew something was wrong," Butras said. "Why didn't you tell me sooner. Oh, by the way, if you let me pass through, my horn might miraculously get quiet again."

He wasn't tense. Nothing was upset inside him. There was a lot I was going to have to learn to get through the year, I thought.

Butras rolled up his window. "God, I hate these people," he said. "Town's gone crazy since that lynching. There's one protest or another every day. The lynching started it. It wasn't like this before."

●

THIRTY days later, New Year's Eve, Wednesday night, the Knicks were at the Garden against the 76ers, just across the bridge in the city. Everyone in Pompan was watching cable, or listening to the radio, pissed that they still blacked out home games. The Knicks had their last shot at the title with Ewing getting older. They were playing like crazy men for Van Gundy.

I liked driving the squad car even though it didn't have an AM dial Butras and I could catch the Knicks on. Every time I thought about the Knicks I couldn't get over the fact that Ewing was a rookie when I was in fifth grade; that he was near retirement and still pulling in 7.5 million a year for his sixteen points, ten rebounds. The car radio had a microphone attached to a silver horseshoe that hung from the dashboard just over the lighter. I never thought I'd enjoy the big round Cavalier, a power car. I liked driving it any speed I wanted up roads marked No Trespassing, up private roads. I hadn't worried about speed in a month. No more tickets for me. If a state trooper pulled me over when I was in my own car, I'd take out my wallet with the picture of me and the Governor at the Academy on graduation day. The Governor had his arm around me and was smiling after a lunch of rubber chicken and peas.

In the month of December, I had grown to enjoy feeling menacing- the heavy pistol, the sharp siren whine, the blue lights gyroscoping, making people dizzy. It was the same feeling that I got when I was weight training. I didn't speak much about this pleasure of my job; I didn't want to jinx it.

Night-riding was best, gliding through Pompan. Shark Chevrolet, a fish-car that could belly flop up a curb, that could take the sandy roads out past Thomas Jefferson Middle School, a car that never broke down, a car that still had power at 80 miles per hour. I liked that the seats were flat black and burned through my starchy white shirts on sunny days, even in the winter.

Butras always had some remark that would snap me out of my drifting. He needed to keep the night passing. December 31st had already been a busy night so he was lively, jumpy. Like me, he had grown up in the town, and not in one of the big houses in the Winthrop Hill area either. I had grown up five blocks away from him, not far from his own Johnston Road.

After dinner at D'Angelo's, I let him drive. I could see the road clearly enough at night but everything was a little blurry when there were oncoming headlights. It had been that way since I started driving at sixteen, even with glasses. I saw the fuzzy halos sometimes around street signs, around porch lights or headlights. Night vision.

Most evenings, very few people called. We just drove and listened to the dispatcher call in fires and rescues. At times, the job seemed like one endless drive, without purpose, nothing much to see, an unthinking kind of emptiness. I kept notes in my head, things to think about when I got in from our shift at 1 AM. I'd light the candles by my bed, put some jazz on the radio, and stare into the dark thinking of my night and of Clarise.

Whenever I asked Clarise if she loved me, she said, "What's your name again?" and pushed at my chest. Then she said, "You're okay for a man."

I was planning to see her after my shift, drive into the city when I got off at midnight, New Year's.

Pompan, New Jersey was a perfect rectangle on the county map, four miles by eight miles. New housing tracts on the north side past the shopping area called The Plaza were mostly unfinished, interrupted by the bad economy, but the houses that had gone up were huge, with pillars beside the front doors, so unlike the other parts of town where the homes were small and vinyl-sided. I had grown up in one of the small, neat houses near the other small shopping area, Oak Lane. The Hudson River was three miles away and sometimes you could smell it like a greasy meal. Across the river in the city was Clarise.

Butras hated that the car was always hotter than the weather. December was his season. All year he waited for the cold. He was the kind of guy who sweated everywhere he went; if you bumped into him, you'd be surpised by how wet he was. He liked being out of the car, on foot, cold but sweating still.

"I feel like taking my shirt off, don't you?" he would ask me on the coldest nights.

"No way."

"You'd still have one of those priss T-shirts on underneath, wouldn't you? It's winter here. Love it or leave it."

It had been a difficult month together locked in the car, a difficult New Year's Eve so far, although just the week before it seemed almost as if we had reached some understanding (he didn't shut me down as fast), laughing at some of our disagreements, ignoring others because I was about to become a graduate of the University of Frank Butras. Nearly all I knew about policing in Pompan came from him and he must have thought there was something important about that, about how he'd be the one I'd call for advice when I went out on my own.

On December 31st at 11:45 PM we were taking the usual circling route around town, near Bryant School, the one the white kids of Pompan got bussed to from the richer Winthrop area because of the elementary school overflow. Bryant stood on top of the hill which sloped down to the mostly black neighborhood around Trygon Park. Not many complaints that made it out from dispatch came from down the hill, but this call had come from there, an address just south of Bryant.

When the call came in at 11:45, Butras hadn't spoken to me in over an hour.

The dispatcher said, "Group of kids in dark parkas, wearing hats. Anonymous caller believes one youngster had a gun. Not sure from a distance if it's a toy or real."

When we saw the kids running, Butras put up the headlights. "Some friends of yours," he said.

•

A month earlier, on the last afternoon of November, one of the black reps from the Pompan City Council, Mrs. Ellis, came over to meet me at my father's house. It was a Sunday, sixteen hours before I started as the only black patrolman in Pompan. My father sat on the brown couch under the window, his hands stiff on his knees and Mrs. Ellis sat on the blue chair next to him. My sister Brenda stood near the CD player, staring out the front window over the evergreens, and I stood beside her, overheated, one hand on the bookcase. Mrs. Ellis was about 40 years old and wore an expensive gray suit. She had long straight hair and glossy tangerine lipstick. My father didn't know Mrs. Ellis (she lived across town in a predominantly black neighborhood) and he reported to us before she arrived that he hadn't voted for her in the last Pompan run-off.

My sister gave her a big smile. My father quietly finished his coffee.

"I hear good things about you. Rutgers, right?" she said, giving me a low, sidelong glance, after quickly checking over at my father. "My nephew goes there, my older brother's boy. I guess he's not a boy anymore. Well, I just wanted to welcome you back to Pompan."

"I'm looking forward to starting," I told her. I was respectful but wasn't about to give her much in conversation. I could tell she had not come to meet me; it was her chance to introduce herself to my father, one of the few black lawyers in town. He was heavy-set and bald with a little patch of gray over the ears. I used to tease my mother that we were the only people who had ever seen my father outside a three-piece suit. He had an elegance; he dressed like a minister.

It was so cold the squirrels had stopped running across the electrical lines. The clouds were thin and low and yellow leaves stuck to the curb across the street. On the sill our cat Ajax played with a weak fly he had batted out of the air. Watching his lazy paw made me think of how well I knew this house: the one soft white linoleum square in the kitchen by the back door, the triangular chip missing from the bottom of the bannister that left me with a scar on my chin; the far corner of the living room where the gray carpet peeled up; the hoop attached to the garage, the edges of the backboard now overgrown by vines growing down from the roof. I'd just come in from shooting out there, and under my Carolina baby blue jacket (like a thousand others on campus, I bought it when we embarassed them in the NCAA's two years before), I was slippery with sweat.

"It's wonderful to have one of us working with the police. Especially with all the bad feelings around in some corners," she said, becoming serious. "Since the lynching the air has changed. People don't care about anyone but their own anymore. I've noticed it. People staying in, trying to hide, turning away quickly in public."

I saw that even champions of Pompan like Mrs. Ellis were disturbed. She smiled again. "Most places nobody really notices who the police are. But you're going to be a celebrity." She sipped the Diet Coke my sister had brought her.

"I sure hope not," I answered Mrs. Ellis. If I was lucky, the small attention I was getting would disappear. It embarassed me. Watching my father I remembered things about him that I hadn't thought of since I left home. When I was ten years old, I dropped one of my father's Duke Ellington 78's. Slipped right out of the fraying cardboard jacket and hit the floor with a loud crack. Two halves lying there, perfectly aligned, an inch apart. My father didn't talk to me for three days. Said he didn't talk to careless kids.

"No, I wouldn't be surprised if you had an invitation to dinner at someone's house every night of the week," Mrs. Ellis said.

"That's good. Save him from his own cooking," Brenda answered.

"Your father tells me you're getting your own apartment."

"And not a moment too soon," my sister interrupted, and we all laughed, except my father.

I held back from saying I was tired of living in my father's bleak house the day I returned to it. During school holidays in the last year I hated going home. I challenged his cigars, his television programs, the noise when he ate. It was a haunted house.

When my mother died 14 months before I inherited her heavy wooden box with a metal hinge in which she'd stored an assortment of candles she used to read by. She preferred the flames of two long candles to the lamp beside her bed. In a bowl, she kept a supply of matchbooks she had taken over the years from restaurants. "There is no light better than fire," she said. By 5 PM, when I got in from my day at the Academy, it was dark outside. I'd light a candle in the room I'd grown up in. The rice paper shades I'd put up glowed white from the flame. The fire gave off a sour smell. In the mirror across the room I studied myself, a tall man with high cheekbones and slanting, wide-set eyes, a pointed chin. The weight of the belt, the stiff crease at the knee.

I don't think I'd recognize myself now.

"I'd like you to meet my son when you get settled," Mrs. Ellis said.

"Be glad to. How old is he?"

"He was just thirteen."

"A little man."

"A big man if you ask him. Big for his age. Wants to run with the tough crowd. I hope they won't have him."

"I'd like to meet him." Ajax, hungry from his slow play, leapt down and headed toward the back door. He was also thirteen years old, still a troublemaker, a bird killer. My mother had rescued him from the ASPCA, and he stayed outside longer and longer since she died. Only I could make the clicking noise my mother used to bring Ajax home on days as cold as this one.

"I'll see if I can bring him over some time," Mrs. Ellis said. "Meantime, I was glad to see that you got a little publicity in *The*

Record. You're big news around here for certain folks. Make your father and sister proud. You write that story yourself?"

"Almost seems like it," my sister told her.

•

ON December 2nd, We filled up the squad car at the gas station where Butras' brother worked after school. Butras said, "My brother needs some help and I'm not the one to help him anymore."

"What kind of help?"

"Someone to say 'stay the fuck out of trouble for a change.'"

It was the first time Butras had brought me into his personal life.

"He's been in trouble since our mother died. Before that really. He had learning problems right off and he still can't read right, skips words or leaves them out, doesn't understand things. Anyway, she always helped him get through school. She read with him like an hour a day, every day except his birthday. She read to him two hours then. She died when he was 11 and he just fell apart."

Coming out of the office from the behind the cash register and candy display toward the pumps, he didn't look much like his older brother. Larry Butras was 15 years old, five foot four or so, with pale skin. His eyes were dark and careless, gloomy for a kid's. He had a round face, brown hair buzzed close, and thick eyebrows that met over the bridge of his nose.

He went around to Butras' side, but he looked in at me. "How much you want?" he asked as if we were strangers.

"Ten," Butras answered.

He went back along the car, unscrewed the cap, unhooked the nozzle and began to do his job. Butras leaned out his window, said something to him that I couldn't hear. The boy came over to the window.

"You're on me for that? Give me a break," the boy said.

"You're in trouble more than you should be."

"You got your thing, I got my thing."

"I guess so."

I felt sorry for the boy and for Butras who only saw his brother lowering himself. I'd lost my mother too, but not when I was eleven. I had some sympathy for the kid, but I didn't like his tone.

"You're a cop, I'm a gangster. If you mess with me, I'll fuck you up," Larry said.

"That's what it's about, huh?"

"That's it."

"Being physical."

"If I wanted, I could play the part with you, man. Shake your hand, joke around, answer your questions. I can do that. That's what it's about with you and your father."

"He's your father too."

The boy ignored Butras. "You only need to be polite. Good manners. That's all it takes."

"You have any news?" Butras asked.

"It's none of your fucking business."

"Nice language," Butras said. He and his brother were locked together forever, each in the other's power.

"I got friends," the kid answered, as if he were convincing himself.

"I heard you have a girlfriend," Butras said.

"I got girlfriends. Two or three. But none of them are really my girl-friend. You know. You get home, you call a girl. If she wants to come over, she comes over."

The kid stopped talking and just stared, daring. He had dead eyes and a thick neck.

"Girls are whores," he said.

"You're such a fucked up mess," Butras said.

"*I'm* a fuck-up? Oooh. You're talking like me, now, is that it? Now we're equals, huh? I keep fucking up because I'm good at it. It's my way. I start fucking-up, I keep fucking up."

"I don't understand what you're saying."

"I don't understand what *you're* saying." He mimicked his older brother. "You think I'm dumb, don't you. You're saying I'm dumb."

"I'm trying to figure out how to help you."

"You're driving around with a dumb, black piece of shit they put on the police force because of the lynching. That makes a lotta sense. How you doing with your new friend there?" he asked sarcastically. "This town is fucked up. "

He turned and walked back to the gas tank, pulled out the nozzle and came back to the window.

"Ten dollars, *bro*," he said. This time, I saw there was more of a likeness between them than I first thought, a flicker in the eyes, a frown.

As we drove away Butras said, "My father should have sent him to military school. Right off. Outta here. He should have done it when Larry was twelve."

"Why didn't he?"

"He must not have believed what he was hearing."

"What was he hearing?"

"That his son was a bum. That his son was a criminal." Butras told me about how his brother had been breaking into houses, stealing cars, buying things on other people's credit cards for the last few years.

"So now what's the plan for Larry?"

"I got this friend and he's always telling me you can't help some kids. You put 'em in a room with a therapist or a social worker or a cop, what have you, and you let them try to solve their own problems, or you try to scare them. And all that happens is the kid has a good laugh. That's my brother. I never had any results with him."

I said, "He's young."

"He's sunk already," Butras said.

•

GETTING in Butras' face at ten o'clock on New Year's Eve set a bad tone. It was a mistake. Getting personal, getting into his life. But when you share a car five days a week, eight hours a shift, you have a lot of time to talk, and I often got the feeling that I was asking too many questions or expressing myself too freely. Things came out, things I shouldn't have said.

Butras, with his seniority, had chosen the first half, four to twelve PM, starting in the sunlight and ending in the dark. That was his choice of shifts and I was with him. I would have taken mornings if it were my choice. But it wasn't. Butras, after all, was an experienced patrolman, and he didn't want to hear anything from a rookie. He had no interest in being a detective; he didn't like change. He liked his job; he liked his shift. Most of the hours we spent together were in the dark, sun setting at 4:30, seven o'clock feeling like midnight.

I never thought that Butras might become a friend. It would be easier when we worked separately, didn't share a car. I imagined a few months ahead when he'd be in his car and I'd be in mine and we'd pull up next to each other and shoot the shit. You couldn't be sure about Butras though- inscrutable in his intense way, not much contact with anyone; a few of the other guys had said the same about him.

Butras told me during our first week together, "I was voted most friendly in my high school class, but I don't really have any friends. Or maybe I just have a different idea of friendship than everybody, and what have you. I got my family and they're my friends, friends in that deep way, the way I mean."

But there were moments when I felt like I could really get along with Butras. Some nights seemed intimate almost, if only for being out in the new snow. We were the first to see it come down, thick flakes, fast in the high street lamps, the sky a strange gray-orange. Some nights in December he actually stopped the car on the edge of the golf course woods to watch it fall and drift, the first storms of the season.

Butras would end every shift by shooting back to the station on Route 6. On the flat stretch between the Bell and Cumberland Avenue exits, he'd slow to 15 miles per hour in the right lane, turn on his high beams and his siren, and try to hit 60 mph in five seconds or less. As we accelerated, the car had a current that connected us, and though I was silent during this ritual, I knew these were the moments I'd remember.

Ten o'clock New Year's Eve, when I spoke, I was thinking to myself: Don't bring it up; leave it alone; maybe later, after we'd celebrated my getting my own car, after we'd had a few beers and watched some football.

But he had gotten me involved, telling me the little he had about his father and brother, refusing to talk with me about the lynching. I said what was on my mind that night. He did the quick tip of his neck to the right, getting the cartilage to snap, his habit when things were bothering him.

•

I was planning to go into the city those first hours of the New Year to see Clarise. We planned to hang at some party, do some dancing like she always wanted me to.

She was dark brown and I felt like I had to see her every day. I had this one picture of her naked, coming out of a lake, her hair all glistening and her round body beautiful. She was walking up toward me when I snapped it. There were black rocks at her feet and the water in the background looked choppy. There was a little surprise on her face, but also her assuredness; she wasn't unhappy that I wanted her on film like that. I kept the photo in my kitchen drawer and I looked at it every night and every morning. I'd been with Clarise on and off for three years and I never got rid of that picture. I needed to look at her. It was the size of my palm but my hands got heavy holding that picture. Sometimes, when I was alone in my room, I'd trace her bones in the darkness.

There was nothing better in the world than Clarise saying, "I like that." The way her tongue slipped out from behind the final "t". When I thought of Clarise, I thought of her body and my body. I thought of her stepping out of her clothes. When I thought of Clarise, I thought of her long red tongue moving in slow circles.

When I first told Clarise that I was starting at the Academy, we were in her apartment on Ft. Washington and 171st Street, upper Manhattan near the medical school she was about to start. It was a Saturday morning and she was in her little kitchen, the size of the serving area in the back of an airplane, and we both couldn't fit in so I was sitting in a chair just outside the door, in the living room, looking in at her over my newspaper. It took three lamps to light her living room, its one window facing the airshaft that spiked the center of the building. Clarise said I was the only person she knew who actually liked that dark room. I didn't mind the dust that rolled up to my feet all the time, little balls that drove her crazy because she couldn't get rid of them. The bedroom, just past the blue couch, led out to a fire escape where we'd sit and have beer in the sunshine listening to the Yankees, watching the bald heads and hat tops of people walking just below us.

In the kitchen, she had her back to me. She'd turned her right knee in and her ankle tipped out. She was wearing a short black one-piece dress and I could see the crease behind that knee, the tip of her elbow as she poured the water. Her hair was up off her neck and I imagined licking the back of each ear.

"You know how in college we were always talking about success, about making a name," I said.

"That only mattered to you," she said. She had a low, crackling voice, a voice with glass in it.

"I think I got the answer," I went on.

"You always got some answer. Go ahead."

"I'm gonna be a detective in five years."

"You know that sounds sort of funny to me," Clarise said with a little snort. "You hardly sleep as it is. How are you going to be police *and* get to Atlantic City twice a month *and* see me? "

"Well you *know* I'm not giving up on Atlantic City," I said.

"No," she said sarcastically. "Wouldn't want them casinos to go out of business, which they'd have to do if you stopped visiting with your money."

It was our mutual friend Bob Esah who told me about the lynching. He came up to me at the Roche library just before graduation with a photograph in his hand.

"You're from Pompan, aren't you?" Bob asked.

"Grew up there. My father is still over there."

"Nice place," he said sarcastically. I didn't know why he had that tone to his voice.

Bob had this weird flap under his upper lip that made him look like he had two upper lips when he smiled. Once a week, he'd take off for Atlantic City. Sometimes I went with him senior year. His brother's girlfriend was a manager at the Trump Taj Mahal. We'd stay up all night playing blackjack in the bright lights, then she'd comp us a room at 6 AM so we could sleep for a few hours before driving back to school.

"I don't spend much time in Pompan anymore," I told Bob.

"Good thing," he said.

He handed me the photo from the front page of the *New Brunswick News*. Black and white, shadowy, taken at night, it showed a figure hanging from the branch of a tree. The head had a strange droop to the left. There was a second figure on the ground next to him wearing a pointed black hat. At first, the photo looked like a Halloween window display.

"Bad stuff," Esah said. "Now *there* is one guy who's seen better days."

"Looks like mannequins," I said. Esah gave me a Don't-be-stupid face.

"Not exactly," he said. "Lynching. Someone left a little mannequin in a KKK outfit, but all dressed in black. Pompan, NJ is about to get overrun."

"Pompan?"

"You bet. Your hometown."

"But that's a white guy, isn't it?" I asked. Bob was a white guy.

"He was. Now he's just a gray guy," he said.

After the lynching, Clarise never liked the idea of my going back to Pompan.

"If you want to solve that lynching, you don't need to be a policeman," she said again as she turned to me in her kitchen. "Why don't you become a reporter or something?"

"I don't want to solve the lynching. That's not gonna happen, I understand that much." I was lying; of course I wanted to find out who did it. But I knew I'd been hired in part to show people that Pompan didn't have a race problem. Not on their police force certainly.

"Cage, I know you've wanted to be a policeman forever, but you still don't know anything about *being* one. You'll have to wear a uniform everyday," Clarise said, coming over to sit on my knees.

"You wear a uniform everyday."

"I wear a white coat."

"That's a uniform."

"Don't be so smart."

"But you *do* wear a uniform."

Looking toward New Jersey that night, the moon we saw from her window was red, lodged in the space between two highrises. Clarise called it a lovers moon. Windows across 171st Street were also open to the cold, people leaning out, staring west toward Pompan toward that wild moon, and I was surprised how close the next building felt, how we could almost touch those neighbors. Someone was playing gospel music and the voices were distant and deep, as if they were coming from the sky. When Clarise touched me later in the dark I almost couldn't feel it, because of the cold, or the the moon, or the excitement.

•

EVERYONE had been expecting snow on New Year's Eve, but it didn't come. As we drove toward Bryant School, the car window was open for Butras and the heat was on. The air outside smelled of dry trees, frozen leaves.

I was thinking, Why aren't these kids home? I was thinking, Why did we have to get this call at 11:45? Fifteen more minutes and I'm home and it's a new year. I was wondering, black kids or white kids here by Bryant?

The kids were in a pack, swerving smoothly. Skinny as fish, in and out of the lights, flashing. There were four or five of them in wool caps. A few of the bigger kids were out front.

I put on the blue lights to scare them.

No one stopped.

Butras gave a shot on the siren. He should have run the car right at them, up the curb, over the blacktop, trying to press them, in the head-lights, up against the school wall. Full speed. Scare the little bastards to a stop like deer.

Two fell back and one stumbled turning the corner of the school building. The last one stopped in a shadow. Must have thought he was out of sight. Invisible.

There was no such thing as a normal traffic stop anymore. Everyone drove without a license or registration; a lot of people had guns under the seats and in the glove compartments. It took about fifteen minutes to learn this. And there was no such thing as a normal kid.

When we came to a stop, our headlights intersected the glare from the floodlight that hung from the side of Bryant School. The last kid from the pack stood at the edge of where the two lights aimed and collided in brightness. The kid stood in the dark, a shadow on the edge of the light. As I got out from inside the car, the air was cold and quiet, except for a gritty scraping.

The kid was approximately twenty yards away from the car. I had reason to believe that a kid like that, even one so small, but one who had been running in a pack away from a police car had a weapon. Still, I couldn't judge his age, the shadow was so small. I couldn't see clearly from that distance. The nearby street lamp had a burn-out bulb. There was no traffic on Lincoln or Hillside.

The top of the kid's head was the perfect curve of a ball because of the hat. A perfect round target. He was only moving a little. I heard the scraping again. I thought it was an animal sound, maybe a squirrel. But the scraping was coming from the kid. The kid could not keep his feet still.

That was the problem of the night: not knowing who's there and at the same time having to put together why they're there. I came out of the car with my gun drawn. I aimed where the lights aimed. Right at that line between the darkness and the light where the kid had stepped out.

I was going to be twenty-three years old in two weeks. I had never shot at a person although I'd thought about it a lot since becoming a policeman, really since I was a boy, my toast bitten into the shape of a gun. If that kid didn't move there'd be no need for me to shoot. There had been a few times in my life when I'd been angry enough to want to kill someone. Wasn't that true for everyone?

I didn't believe people who said they never wanted to kill someone. They were liars. Sometimes people have to lie.

I was struggling for breath. I couldn't get my breath. I wanted to talk, call, scream, but I couldn't.

My throat closed and it felt as if only vomiting would open it again.

●

THE details of New Year's Eve will always come back to me in ways that it won't to those reporters who must have arrived early the next morning trying to get the full story, making the mistake of thinking they could get the whole story. Forgetting how strange some stories can be. Forgetting that some stories don't make sense.

Every thought I have is shaded by guilt and rage. I feel as if I owe that kid or myself something, but I don't know what. I can't catch the shape of what I owe, only the feeling. But I need to know. Or maybe I'm just deceiving myself.

My mother died in a room like this one. My father, whose silence was devotion, was with her. How many deaths have there been in this room? I don't know how Clarise will do her medical work, being so close to death every day.

My mother used to say I was like her father, because I never made any trouble. Growing up, when things went well for me, she would tell me about my grandfather, dark-skinned and wrinkle-headed, a man I never met. I was left-handed like he was, same color, same quizzical expression, like I was always looking for answers, she said. During a visit home three years ago when she first got sick, I told my mother I'd gotten an A in Criminology. "You could never even write a term paper in high school, you remember? Didn't have the interest. But thank God. Goes to show, you got a passion, you do the work," she said, smiling. "You will be some good policeman Officer Gambell. Fits your disposition. Asking everyone except yourself questions."

She meant it in fun, of course, so I answered her in the spirit of fun, "You know better than anyone that I already got all the answers." I knew it would make her feel good when I became a detective, like her brother, her father's son.

●

ON Wednesday December 3rd, we were touring the Lincoln Hill area, when a black BMW ran a stop sign at Berry and Appleton.

"Watch this," Butras said. "He shouldn't be driving wildly in this neighborhood. I mean, I don't like that. There are kids around and what have you. I'm gonna scare the shit out of him."

"Okay."

"Take notes. You can do the next one."

Butras put on the flashing light and accelerated, taking a left onto Appleton. The houses were close together on either side, hoops over garages, front doors open, parents coming home at 7 PM. There were a few little dips in the road and the guy probably didn't see us until we were right up on him. He was doing about 30 in a 15 zone.

"He's a yuppie," Butras said. "He's probably not that bad a guy, but I'm gonna have to shake him up because I can't have him driving around here like that."

Butras gave one pull on the siren and the guy looked in his rear view coming up out of a gully and pulled over where the road levelled.

"I'll leave my door open and talk loud so you can hear how it's done," he said and got out briskly.

The driver was already rolling down his window and through the dusk I saw the resigned look on his face.

Butras got up to his car and stopped short of the driver's window and asked for his license and registration I could tell, but I really couldn't hear anything else with our car still running and the twenty feet between us. When the guy handed over his papers, Butras moved up next to him and bent over and talked close to his face for a moment, then came back toward our car and got in.

"You heard me, right?"

"No. The motor was on," I answered.

"The guy lives around here. He's not a bad guy, he's not too much of an asshole. He's a resident here. He says he was just rushing home to see his family. He says that he hasn't seen them in a few days and he didn't notice anyone coming when he went through the sign. I explained to him that there are kids around here and it's pretty dark and you got to move slower, and I think he's pretty upset; he feels pretty bad. He was real apologetic. So I'm not going to give him a ticket. Why ruin his life?"

"Why not?" I asked.

"Why should I? Why should I be a jerk? This way he'll think police are OK. You're good to people, they'll be good to you."

Hanging around the station I learned pretty fast that there are cops who when they're out of uniform are different from the way they are in uniform. And you have those cops who are the same in and out of uniform. Butras was the first kind; he was actually friendlier in his uniform, a little sullen out.

•

CLARISE insisted that I talk about my mother's death. Her urgency made me pull further away and I'd end up working on my motorcycle instead of speaking—blue metal, silver in my hands—knowing that Clarise was studying my back. Being watched by her brought me pleasure, but there was tension in the silence.

My mother's brother Harold taught me about bikes, riding into town on one fifteen years ago. Uncle Harold wore his hat, his preacher get-up; underneath, a shaved skull; he had a magnetic field for me, everything bent around him, he was a mood shifter. I was reluctant to tell my mother how I felt about Harold, just as I was reluctant to talk to Clarise about my mother.

Harold's Harley had a sticker: "Blame nobody. Expect nothing. Do something." He was a detective in Detroit, and he defined my mother for me—freeing her, tapping into her creativity when he came to town. The first time I met him (I was eight) after his thousand mile ride to New Jersey, Harold said, "Hotshots call me so many vile names that it's almost respect," and I had to ask my mother what vile was. She laughed like mad, the way she did when Harold was around. My father stayed in his study and worked. He had no use for Harold and his motorcycles.

Harold sent me books when I was in high school, sensational police cases. When we spoke on the phone, he told me to snatch the paperback murder mysteries my mother was always reading and to try to solve them. He read them along with me, half a continent away, and we'd go over the clues together. Harold knew that my father would never be resigned to having a cop for a son, he knew that my father thought it was a waste, that thirty years ago things had been different for Harold than they were for me now. Harold talked to my father when he knew I was serious.

"You want me to be a cop?" I asked Harold, senior year of high school.

"If it fits," was all he answered.

Four years later, Harold didn't understand when I told him I couldn't come out to Detroit where he wanted to get me started. Clarise was starting medical school in New York, I said, and I was going to stay around her, take a job in Pompan, hoping for a patrolman's job in New York where there was a 2-year wait list for the Academy. Harold had been married three times. He believed bad luck came in threes, and a cop never put a woman first.

There was never a time I imagined being anything other than a policeman. And so when I *was* one, I thought the secrets of policing would be quickly revealed to me only because I'd already imagined them, thought I'd seen them in Harold.

•

THE night after the lynching, I called Ethan instead of my father. I thought to myself: If Ethan hasn't been changed by the lynching, then Pompan hasn't been changed either. He was the one guy from high school days I kept up with who still lived in Pompan. He and his parents lived behind us. Growing up, I'd head out our back door, pass the crabapple tree that supplied us with ammunition for spring-time fights, cross our back lawn and cut through the hedges to play ball on the Bing's driveway.

He'd given me the nickname Cage when I was nine years old, saying that when he saw me in the screened-in porch at the back of our house (where we ate dinner in the summer), it looked like I was in a cage.

His father had coached him into the third best 14-and-under tennis player in the East. Ethan, this little black kid with skinny legs and this wild, sliding forehand, was a tennis star when we were growing up. I remember him walking around the court telling himself back then to "hit the ball at 5 o'clock. Hit the ball at 5 o'clock." He saw the ball like the face of a clock and he told me that he wanted to hit every forehand on the outside to spin it into the court. I never got what he was talking about because I didn't play tennis, but I saw him play plenty of times, winning the town tournament against all the grown-ups, getting to the state finals. I rode along with him and his father to some faraway tournaments at these fancy clubs where everyone was white and wore white and drank iced tea with mint, where the clay was swept between sets with a long, two-handled broom, and Ethan, wearing his game face and black skin, was treated like visiting royalty.

But he stopped growing at age 13. At 5 foot 5 inches his serve didn't continue to pick up speed and his father rode him mercilessly trying to make up for size with drilling. Ethan started losing to kids he'd always beaten and his father stopped driving him to tournaments. Ethan had never been one to laugh much, but now he was demoralized and shamed. He quit the high school team and his father stopped talking to him. He started missing school and I never saw him much, even on weekends.

When I went to Rutgers, Ethan stayed home. His mother had seizures and Ethan had always been the one to care for her. Despite taking medicines, she was prone to relapses. I saw it happen only once. I was 12 or 13 and it was near dinner time on a fall evening as I was coming through the hedge. I saw Mrs. Bing carrying two brimming A&P bags in her arms when she fell and lay on the ground shaking, the red milk container splitting open into a white puddle that settled around her at the base of the basketball pole. At the sound of her bags ripping, I saw Ethan and his father come to the back window overlooking the driveway. I remember Mr. Bing's face, weirdly angry and discouraged. Only Ethan came out for her, a rag in his hand. He knelt beside his shaking mother, put his left hand under the back of her head, and tried to stuff the rag into her chattering mouth. I knew he missed a tournament once because his right hand had been badly bitten during one of her attacks.

I'd always believed Ethan thought of himself as his mother's only hope for a cure. When I met up with him during college, we'd shoot around in his driveway and he'd ask me about school in this quiet voice, but not say much about himself. I knew he was in trouble in some large sense, and he knew it too. My advice felt useless and he seemed to be expecting some terrible resolution to his problems. Still, I always called him at Christmas and for his birthday.

When I got him on the phone the night Bob Esah told me about the lynching, Ethan talked cautiously, as if I were a threat. It wasn't Christmas day or his birthday.

"You heard about the lynching?" I asked. I assumed everyone had, but I could never be sure with Ethan.

"Couldn't help but hear, you know," he said.

"What's the word around there on it?" I asked.

"I don't hear much."

"Anyone we know get a visit from the FBI?"

"I don't know anyone," he said.

He sounded drugged and I didn't pursue the subject. I asked about his Mom and if he'd been following any sports, then our conversation wound down.

"Why are you calling me, Cage?" he finally asked.

"Just checking up," I said. I was worried about him. Bad things had happened since he dropped out of sight. He had gotten spinal meningitis, and his aunt was killed in a commuter airplane crash.

"That's good of you," he said.

•

IN the first days after the lynching, plenty of theories were rolled out. The victim was a drunk, a derelict, a pervert. It was a drug hit. The killing was done by a violent wing of the Nation of Islam. It was group of white militia who thought the hanging man had been a black-lover and so they left him out next to a black mannequin to teach him an eternal lesson. It was some radical black group that was setting itself up as a new inverted KKK; now the targets were white people. This last theory was the one that lingered.

"Any leads on the Pompan story?" I asked Bob Esah a few days after the lynching. I thought he would have inside information from working on the *Rutgers Daily*.

"Police there don't know what the fuck's going on," Bob said. "This murder was way over their heads. They're just a bunch of half-educated hometown guys looking to have a quiet life and then retire. Of course they all want to figure it out. Be a hero. But here's the problem. They're all white. And the lynching was done by blacks."

"That's the word?"

"That's what a lot of people, including me, think."

"No proving that though?"

He ignored me. "You probably know some of those cops. Boys from your school days."

"Probably."

"It hasn't been that long since you've been gone."

Bob didn't know that as a boy I worked at all varieties of trouble around Pompan. Even then, Pompan was expanding into the

Meadowlands, gas stations and Burger Kings rising on landfill. The southern part of town became directly connected to the Garden State Parkway so drugs entered easily. I stayed away from crack but high on marijuana I once stole animals from their classroom cages and let them go into the onion grass of Toca Loca Park. I snapped off the side mirrors of cars. Petty stuff, and there was never an eyewitness. Even then, I knew you could get addicted to trouble if you weren't careful, that sooner or later you'd get caught.

"You've had a photograph of that hanging man up since the night it happened. Everyone's a little worried about you," Bob said.

"Good picture, huh?"

The photo of the hanging man (taped below one of Clarise and one of my mother on the refrigerator) had become a dominant presence in my life in those days. There'd been no capture or explanation. The Mayor of Pompan hinted in print about the FBI's arrogance and ineptitude.

In the picture, the man was hanging in a square marked off by police tape like he was an animal in a zoo exhibit. I imagined him helpless and disoriented and beaten just before he died. I imagined his death to be like what happened to Mrs. Bing during her seizures. Then all he was was an empty stare at the ground and a hopeless weight. Bugs finding their way into his body.

I thought of the rope like a leash on an animal. He was heavy with flesh, gravity pulling at him.

If I looked for too long at the picture, it made me feel sick.

Some days I looked at the picture and thought, If I don't go home something awful will happen again there.

People who came by the house my best friend Cedric and I shared at school glanced quickly at that photo. It must have had them worried, two black men with a picture of a lynched white man in the middle of the kitchen. I felt some eyes stay on me longer than they used to, eyes that turned away when I stared back. I felt I had to maintain my composure in the face of outrage; how could they just look at that man and say nothing? Why didn't everyone have this picture up?

Maybe they were just thinking: why does that photo get at Gambell so bad? To this day, I don't know exactly, although I know it only reinforced my desire to go back to Pompan. It wasn't that I had a fascination with horrors in general, only with that lynched man. The more I think about it now, the more I realize that my interest in returning to Pompan came from the feeling that my memory had betrayed me. When I thought of my life in Pompan not so long before, I recalled a pretty good childhood, not one broken by fears, but one that included some foolish things, some romance, some crazy nights out with the boys. Nothing hopeless or hateful. No lynching.

And now this hanging *was* Pompan.

Had I missed something?

From the beginning, I had the feeling that the lynchers weren't going to get caught. I had the feeling that this would be a mystery in Pompan for the next twenty years, one that would drive people away, or keep children inside, or cause sudden fistfights in supermarket aisles.

•

WHEN I told Brenda that I was coming back to Pompan, the night after I told Clarise and Cedric, she said, "I wish you'd police your father. Now there's a man who needs some policing."

My older sister had always lived in Pompan. Brenda lived three blocks from my parents, and ever since my mother died, she'd gone over and cooked dinner for my father twice a week. She specialized in rice and beans, "healthy food" she called it, which my father had probably gotten used to. When she wasn't cooking for him, she must have been eating a lot of unhealthy because she was up around 200 pounds. I didn't talk to her about her weight anymore; she was a grown woman with a nasty temper. The last time I tried she yelled at me, "What do you know about what I eat? Nothing. For your information, I've tried every shit-tasting diet out there—the all-grapefruit diet, the protein shake routine, the weight watchers. I exercise more than you, and here I am. Nothing wrong with the way I am."

Brenda was a big girl and she beat on me mercilessly when we were small. She slapped me around until I was twelve and then she stopped and made out like she had done me a favor, toughening me up.

When my father started dating a younger woman, a white woman, it left a sour taste with Brenda. My sister had a network of spies around Pompan—she'd been popular in high school, still worked in the Pompan school department, and kept up with people—girls she knew in high school who now worked in groceries and waitressed in restaurants and owned flower shops around town, and there was little news of my father that didn't reach her. She was relentless in her need to know every story about our father and in her need to share them with me. I didn't really care who he was dating and I told Brenda so. She was worried that he was making a fool of himself seeing a woman so soon after Mother died.

Brenda told her boyfriends that family was her greatest pleasure. But it was our father whom she was attached to; Brenda had nothing good to say about our mother until she died.

I couldn't imagine my father making a fool of himself. He never hesitated to use his charm on people and usually got what he wanted. At the start of my new job he made it clear that he didn't like the idea of me working with the Pompan police. I thought perhaps he just didn't want me nearby too, watching; Brenda was bad enough.

•

EVERY Saturday morning at Rutgers, Cedric went fishing. His cousin had started taking him when he was six years old, plucking him out of East Orange and the cement, and Cedric remembered catching that first slapping mackerel like it was yesterday. "Goddamn that was a beautiful fish. I kept it in the refrigerator in a plastic bag for weeks but it started to stink and my mom tossed it out one day when I was at school," he once told me. Every Saturday he was out of our room by 4 AM catching a bus south to the Jersey shore. Most days he'd come back with striped bass that he'd prepare for his dinner. Cedric cleaned the fish right in our sink, slit open the bellies and let the guts run onto some newspapers he put down. Then ran his finger along the inside, rinsed out the last blood, and threw it on a Hibachi he took out of the closet, the little eyes shrinking in the heat. I never touched the stuff. It smelled like oil burning in a car engine.

When I complained, Cedric said, "You've lost touch with the hunter in you. You've lost touch with hardship."

"I never had hardship. That's you, man," I answered.

Freshman year, Cedric built curves into the corners of our room.

"Africans don't live in square rooms," he said.

"You're from East Orange, not Mali," I told him.

Cedric had grown up on the city pavement and never really got used to the quiet of the woods around the school, the electric buzz of the streetlight just outside the window of the house we rented senior year, the cricket quiet of the neighborhood interrupted by silverware crashing and our next door neighbor's maniacal laugh. The man collected antlers and we could see them through his side window.

For one year we shared that big old house with the automatic broom the owners left behind and the ceiling fan in the living room. Cedric had a banner on the wall above his bed that read: Work Is For People Who Don't Fish. His room was filled with his fishing stuff—poles and reels and lines and hooks.

I always thought it was strange that despite all his fishing, Cedric had these smooth, soft hands. They were almost feminine with perfect round nails. Before Cedric, I had this picture of serious fishermen having ripped-up fingers.

Cedric was the only one who took as much interest in the lynching as I did. We talked about it every day, even when the news about the hanging man wasn't news anymore. He was hanged from a tree out in the woods behind the sixteenth green of the public golf course on the north edge of town; he was hanged by his own belt and had been dead about eight hours when he was found, purple-faced and limp.

When Cedric first saw the picture of the lynched man he said, "Badness. The dude had *his* moment of truth."

"No pity?" I asked.

"I'm not the judge or the executioner," Cedric answered.

Bob Esah, who'd been listening, said to Cedric, "You don't take any shit, do you."

"Not from Cage," he said. "You? Yeah I'd take shit from you."

●

AT Bryant, I no longer thought of the shape in front of me as a person; it was a shadow. I watched for the shadow to make a dash for it. To the left into the dark. To the right into the lights. I couldn't guess which way.

I thought: How futile it is for this shadow to run. It can't outrun my gun.

I thought: Shadow, don't you move. Spare us both.

I watched for other shadows.

The weather had changed three times that day. In the morning there was a cold, slicing rain. Later, the sun came out, drying the ground fast, leaving a surprising warmth. Then it chilled down in the late afternoon. They were predicting snow.

It was a pearly sky. It was an everlasting sky. I wanted to go home. I wanted to climb into bed, talk with a warm Clarise.

At 11:50 PM, ten minutes before the end of our shift, when I got out of the squad car, it took a minute for my eyes to adjust. Two great maples stood on either side of the school, their leaves gone, framing the wall with the light sprayed on it. I was trembling. I was cold. I was not thinking really. I had no words. I could not think of the word *stop*. It was surprisingly quiet.

The shards of light. Too little sleep. I was having a hallucination. Small things looked huge. The sky had closed in, compressing the air around me, pressing on me.

Our car was half in the street and half on the curb. Its lights were angled slightly upward at the wall. There was a patch of grass between the sidewalk and blacktop and the wall where the small figure, the shadow, stood.

I was cold and I was sweating around my collar.

●

RETURNING to your hometown is going back to your past. When I first came back to Pompan I would drive past the yellow house I grew up in. There were matching evergreens in front that needed to be trimmed every few months or they'd block the windows on either side of the front door. There was a small square of grass in front of each evergreen that ran all the way down to the sidewalk. The Japanese maple tree my mother planted when I was born was now full grown, an umbrella of thin branches.

As long I could remember my father had collected Ellington records. There had been jazz in the house when I was growing up. Old 78's with that grainy sound like someone was pouring rice in the background. My parents' big Victrola, fifty years old, with a heavy curved playing arm and a wide hood that closed like a casket. After inheriting the Victrola from her parents, my mother refused to get a modern stereo. "Who needs it?" she said as she danced around the living room in her long dark skirts and a scarf thrown around her neck.

I couldn't imagine my father in there alone, putting on lights, cooking himself a fried egg, turning on a TV. I thought of our whole family in the living room when I was a boy: my mother on the floor with us playing some board game, my father's chair turned slightly away from the center. That position meant he was thinking out some deep problem and he would rejoin the activity when the problem was solved.

When Brenda told me he'd been spotted in recent months in a bar-restaurant where the lights were kept low, drinking from butterscotch water glasses with his new woman friend and sitting in a corner booth past the space set aside for dancing, I thought he had given in to the loss of my mother in a way he wasn't facing. My sister had broken up with her long-time boyfriend Lucas (who she never married, for unclear reasons) and was concentrating her full attention on our father, or rather was making sure (in her words) he wasn't "slumming" with "comical-looking" women.

I couldn't imagine the three of us—my sister, father and me—in the same town again. The thought of being close to my sister wasn't exactly a bonus to the Pompan police job. Nor was plotting against my father.

He and I had never gotten along. He'd always been a man who felt sure, beyond any shadow of a doubt, of all that he did. I dreaded seeing him when my little league team lost, when I got "C" in ninth grade English, when I bought myself fancy sneakers. My friends admired my father and came to our house to hear him tell stories about his college baseball days, his war experiences. Stories that he never bothered to tell my sister or me who had only a superficial knowledge of his past.

I never brought any girls home to meet him. I used to think it was because I was afraid of what he'd say to them. Later, I realized it was because of what he'd say to me *about* them—how they weren't quick enough, or serious enough, or were too quiet.

I was careful never to ask my father for anything. So my father had no right to ask me not to be a cop. If he was going to say anything, my mother must have talked him out of it.

When my mother was sick and I came home from college, I dreaded seeing him even more because all his certainties seemed forced to me. How could he be so full of advice when my mother was losing her hair to chemotherapy?

•

WHEN I was still at the Academy, Brenda told me the rumor that the police didn't care who lynched Clarence Wilbourne; they were glad he was dead. Less work for them, bringing him in drunk every other day, answering some call that he was fighting. I didn't disregard her; she knew everybody and everybody talked to her. Pompan was full of eyes and ears and she was full of hearsay, tidbits supplied to her by school friends. The only two persons she'd never gotten to confide in her were my father and me.

When I started on the force, I made it my business to ask everyone I met their opinion of the lynching. But it was Brenda—whom I'd always believed thought only of food, romance, weekend plans and my father—who offered me the cleanest insights.

"Black man didn't do that lynching," Brenda said. "No black man put out those black mannequins."

Now, two months later, the pain won't let me rest in this white hospital room; it grows hotter and hotter until I dose myself from the pump beside my bed. The secondhand on the electric clock moves like one in my sixth grade classroom, circling slowly across from me; too much time passing. Pain brings on the logic of childhood when all that matters is truth and revenge. But neither is possible anymore. Among the memories that linger as I wake in this morphine haze is what Butras told me when he learned that I'd been asking around the station about the lynching.

"That's before your time. Leave it alone," he said.

"Can't," I told him. "Black people are interested in lynchings, as a rule. Cops too."

Butras' piercing stare set off alarms in my heart. I knew even then that using sarcasm with him was foolish. But at the time I also wondered: what did he care that I was asking questions?

The first week, when I asked Tom Prescott in the squad room about the lynched man, Tom rolled his eyes. "The man was a drunk. Clarence Wilbourne. Spent his whole life in Pompan and nobody liked him. Always in a fight, always getting pulled off someone. Beat up women who for some reason didn't turn him away fast enough. When he was locked up here last time, sobering up, he'd say his life was ruined by a Catholic pedophile priest, but nobody believed him. Listen, in this job, every day, we see men and women doing what they shouldn't be doing. Clarence was the worst.

"When we picked up his son Ronny for the lynching, we knew it was bullshit. We knew he wasn't the one. But the FBI wanted to put an end to the speculation that it was a black on white crime. They wanted it over. We knew Ronny couldn't think clear enough to have arranged that whole scene and lynched his father, although he had reason to. The man beat the shit out of his own kid."

•

THE first few days, I thought about Butras all the time, even at home. He gave me a lot to think about. If I asked him anything, he would talk for minutes, slanting the conversation every which way. It always came back to one or another part of Butras' code of behavior.

"You can't try to jam people. You just can't do that when you're a police officer. They see Frank Butras and they say, 'He's a good guy and he's a policeman. It's pretty nice that he treats people like that.' And then they treat you right. As an officer, you have to be fair and you have to be discreet in a town like this."

I knew that maybe Butras was not one of those white guys who wanted quick acceptance and the only way he knew to get it was to talk nasty, to talk like he thought black people talked to each other, and if he got a friendly enough response, the ice was broken. He was just trying to keep up the conversation.

Butras put the pressure on me to make the choice: you want to find something to argue about today or not? I didn't mind the game. It didn't really bother me. But talking about these conversations with Clarise did, because when I was recounting my day I could feel the coercion, the pressure, from Butras. All the time I figured I could give as good as take, and after a few weeks, when things were better, I wouldn't spend that much time considering the reasons Butras had for giving me shit. All new cops got shit.

On the 4th, I just gave Butras the freeze back for a few hours after he got me really pissed off.

After dinner I finally said to him, "Is it always going to be like this?"

"Like what?"

"You talking through your asshole."

"Yes sir," Butras said, giving me a salute.

I wasn't afraid of Butras. Some days I found myself hoping he'd start a fight with me. Some days it would have pleased me to inflict some pain on his sad face.

•

I lifted five or six days a week after I broke my arm playing flag football freshman year of college. They sent me to the weight room for rehabilitation and I knew immediately that I'd be spending some serious time there. I was lifting every day for my arm, light weights, and I put on six pounds the first year. I kept lifting and put on another six pounds sophomore year, but I wasn't lifting for my arm anymore.

I was addicted to it, I guess. I went at it hard, got my mind off things. The air was hot and stinking and made me want to hurt the machine. Crush it. Mind on the steel and the blood thudding in my ears. I felt like I was flying.

The guys who hung around the gym those first months saw my skinny arm getting bigger and they said, "You have to lift big to get big." That's the motto that gave me a huge boost. I had to constantly remind myself what I was planning to accomplish and then do it. My mind became strong and disciplined. It was a fast sweat for me, and although Cedric assured me it was dull, it wasn't.

The more weight you move for a set number of reps on a particular exercise, the larger your muscles get. That's the fact. For my legs: squats, dead lifts, and leg presses. For my back: chins, pull-downs, pulley rows, shrugs and dead lifts. For my chest: bench press, parallel bar dips, incline presses. For my abdomen: hanging leg raises and crunches. For my arms: wrist curls and barbell reverse curls.

Cedric could never understand why I wasn't at the gym very long, but he just wasn't familiar with lifting. My workouts lasted only about twenty minutes, eight to ten reps per set.

Clarise liked it, liked the way I looked. I heard her bragging on the phone to her friend Cheryl about my arms. She said, "Forearms are the sexiest thing on a man. Above the belt."

When my arm broke, I felt helpless and lifting was the opposite of helpless. During rehab, the moments of my greatest happiness came at the times of the worst pain.

Now I awaken in almost complete darkness, the white sheets glowing, and I think of the weights. My life is in pieces. My father and Clarise and Brenda have given up hope, but they don't remember when I broke my arm freshman year.

•

WHEN I told Cedric that I would be the first black on the Pompan police he said, "Way past 20 and you're still a fool."

He was working at the School for the Deaf in the city. His sister Marna was deaf and he'd learned sign language growing up. He didn't know anything about police departments except not to trust them.

I explained the whole structure to him, the forty people on the force, including two women, a chief, a deputy chief, 6 sergeants, 4 detectives, 1 court officer, 1 safety officer and the rest patrolmen.

"And you're the first nigger," Cedric said.

"Is race always on your mind?" I asked Cedric. I knew the answer.

"It's always in the air."

"Really it's not."

"Mostly it is."

"How?" I asked.

"Nigger, for one thing," Cedric said.

"You hear that much where you are?"

"Oh yeah, in New York City. Word is everywhere."

"Well, not here."

"Course not," Cedric said. "Just lynchings."

•

MOST days, I was quiet with Butras. I was learning; that's what I was there for, to watch and listen. I'd only recently completed the twelve weeks at the Academy. The role-plays, the reaction to violence classes, the constitutional law seminars at Rigan Community College. The sessions out on the farm the Academy owned in the northwest corner of the county were where we learned to drive like policemen, to chase and avoid, learned to plan an escape route when the car in front of you freezes and you have to hit the brake and spin out toward your escape side and while you're fishtailing, accelerate, because if you don't you're dead.

After five years on the force, this stuff was natural to Butras.

Still, I felt superior to Butras. I felt superior to all of them. Brenda said I had too much attitude, too much "psychology." They were going to be street cops in Pompan, New Jersey for the next thirty years; I was going to move up, move into New York.

"They all seem a little dull," I told Clarise on the phone. My phone bill was soaring; I was talking to her every day.

"Dull?"

"Not stupid. I mean tired. They all have gripes and old injuries and they keep talking about a better life. But what's a better life for them? Getting to watch hockey on TV 24 hours a day?"

"Men who watch hockey. I have some of those in my medical school class."

I knew what they were saying about me down at the station: that I'd rather work out or see Clarise than go out for a beer, that I rarely sat down for a cup of coffee with my fellow officers. In the station they kept their eyes on me. Whites who don't spend a lot of time with blacks like to watch us, half from distrust, half from interest in our ways.

I told Clarise that sometimes I was amused by Butras, but also a little irritated that I had drawn as my teacher someone who was always going to give me a hard time. When I looked over, I saw a short guy who was in shape, a guy with a thick wrestler's neck who was balding fast, the blonde hair on top thinning. You could see through to the pink scalp. And when he smiled, his teeth had a sharp, clean look to them.

December was a 31-day month and it was a long way to my first paycheck. In the beginning, I felt apart from Butras and his comments. I wondered why Butras had become a cop, but I didn't ask. There didn't seem to be much joy for him outside his work, but he was always saying there was no job he'd rather have.

•

On Friday the 5th, Mrs. Ellis brought her son by the station at the start of my shift. He was small for his age, maybe 5 foot 2 and dark-skinned. He didn't like having his mom carting him around and I didn't blame him. But he had something close to hatred in his eyes.

"Put your hand out," Mrs. Ellis instructed him. "Show some respect."

"Gambell." The way he used my name, the way he said it looking at the stencil on my shirt pocket, rubbed me wrong.

I saw who he was and squeezed his little hand until I felt the bones shift. Then I pulled him a few steps away from his mother.

"Brother got to be hard to make it in this hard world," I said.

"You here to figure out that lynching?" little Ellis asked, taking a step back toward his mother.

"Who do *you* think did it?" I asked him. Everyone had an opinion, I'd learned since coming back. Except Butras. I'd talked to plenty of people about it and the subject made people hopeless or merciless. Someone had written to the *Record* just that week suggesting all the trees in town get cut down so it didn't happen again. There was a desperate sense in the air that things could never be fixed.

I remembered Ellis's age: a state of contradiction—people loving me and hating me—a bitter taste in my mouth every day.

"Someone had a reason," the boy said.

•

THAT night, I tried again with Butras. We were driving past the golf course, past the tree where it happened. There were six poinsettas in silver foil-wrapped pots next to the bronze plaque that was sunk in the ground.

"Who do you think did it?" I asked.

"A crazy person. A sicko," he said.

"Why don't you think anyone was caught?"

"Whoever did it didn't live around here. Came in, went out."

"Why'd they come here?"

"No idea. Why not? Quiet place."

"No suspects from Pompan?"

"There were plenty but you asked me what I thought," Butras shut me down.

"I don't hear much talk about it at the station."

"No reason to. Nothing good to say. Unsolved mystery."

"Nobody gets killed for nothing."

"Don't concern yourself with that case. Stay focussed on the routine stuff we see everyday."

"How many detectives are still on it?" I couldn't leave the hanging man alone.

"It's an FBI priority, not a department priority any more."

"Why not?"

"Ask the chief."

"I hear the dead man had a lot of enemies."

"The hanging was a surprise, but finding Clarence Wilbourne dead didn't make one person around Pompan blink."

●

I met Cedric for dinner in the city on December 6th, cheap Chinese at House of Lotus. One week of experience under my belt. I told Cedric all I could remember about my first week with Butras.

I told him how Butras never complained about the stress of the job, or its toll on him, about the paper work or the latest regulation. The Chief had passed down the word that we were all supposed to write two traffic tickets a day. If not, overtime pay would be docked or we might get a reprimand. During the day with plenty of drivers out, it was pretty easy to find two tickets; on the night shift it wasn't so easy. The best place to find a broken headlight or a loud muffler, Butras said, was in the poorer section of town, in the black section, southwest.

"He's just getting the job done. Butras talks trash. He's used to talking trash," I said. We were eating shrimp lo-mein, my favorite.

"Cage, the only time you're not black to them is when you're in your bathroom stall and all they can see is your dropped pants," Cedric said.

I changed the subject when Cedric started that routine. "You hear from Clarise?" I asked. She'd dropped out on me again for a few days, not returning my calls.

"She's your girl."

"You know her too."

"Some of the time."

"Same here."

While I wanted to see Clarise all the time she didn't always want to see me. That wasn't new. I knew what was going on: her younger brother had checked in. Carl was a street person in Chicago, a schizo-phrenic who'd gone in and out of mental hospitals for years. The first time I heard about Carl was in Clarise's room during our senior year. (I'd been seeing her for over a year at that point and I knew then that she kept her secrets well.) I saw her face get all stiff when she answered the phone: Carl was calling saying he had a shotgun up to his mouth. "I'm gonna put you out of your misery and kill myself," he told her. I sat next to Clarise for three hours as she begged him not to shoot himself. She begged him and begged him and when she hung up, she cried for three more hours not knowing what was going to happen. The next morning she flew to Chicago where she met her father and they went looking for her brother who they found through the social worker at his regular shelter.

Most of the time I wasn't there when she got one of these calls from Carl, but I knew when Carl had contacted her because she disappeared. She didn't want to see anyone she was close to; instead she'd hang around with people she didn't know well, who didn't know about her brother. Then a week or so later she'd call me up and apologize.

•

BUTRAS' favorite hour of the day was five to six PM and by the second week he got me liking it too. We did the rush-hour crossing at Oak Lane. Commuters were coming home up Lincoln, shoppers were choosing dinner at the A&P, people were buying hardware at Whittier's, getting their dry cleaning, picking up a pizza. We parked in front of the Floss (a sports bar and restaurant with lots of wood paneling) and helped men in ties, spike-headed teenage boys who wore only T-shirts in thirty-five degrees, young married couples gripping each other against falls, tiny Filipino nurses getting their buses for home, and children in long stocking caps to cross the street. In cars, businessmen waited, tie clips still closed, giving hostile, bewildered looks at the pedestrians who slowed them down.

Butras considered this important work—important for public relations—and we spent an hour there just waving the traffic onward and stopping it when a mass of people had collected on the curb. He let drivers turn left out of the A&P lot, and asked high schoolers walking home how the wrestling team was doing. People he'd known since he was a kid came by and asked how his father was, how his brother was.

For this hour, Butras was upbeat, springy, delighted to be at his job. He had become a policeman for this it seemed, to guide, instruct, make order out of a busy intersection. At least for this hour, he controlled the day for his community.

On the eighth, I ran into Roy Verin, an old classmate from Pompan High who I recognized from fifty yards away by his twitching, tipping walk. While I expected to see many faces I recognized when I moved back to Pompan, I didn't. Catching up with Roy was a surprise. His complexion was still bad, cheeks thin and sunken.

"When did you move back to town?" he asked when he recognized me. He kept his face partly lowered when he spoke, just as he had when he was younger. He was looking my uniform up and down.

"Started about a week ago," I said.

"I remember hearing that."

"Big change," I said.

"I don't blame you. It's good to see you back, man. And in uniform. Damn." He let out a short whistle. Roy was the first kid I'd ever seen hit a little league pitch over the fence. Three hundred feet when he was twelve.

"What's happening around here?" I asked.

"You see it. You know about the lynching. Yeah, yeah, course you do. People out of their heads over that. No one cares the dude was white. A lynching is a lynching. White this time, black the next. You weren't here then, were you? Can't talk with people, can't reason with them. No one listens."

"And what's up with you?" I asked Roy.

"Same old, same old. Look man, I'm on my way somewhere. So I'll check you later."

I remembered that Roy never talked about himself; he would change the subject if you asked. He'd escape.

●

THE Beliefs of Bone, a gang that had been at the high school even in my day, had gotten rougher over the past few years. They were recruiting younger and younger kids. They were selling more drugs; they had started setting people on fire with kerosene. They had black spray-painted their "BoB's" under nearly every overpass in Pompan. Some people suspected them of the lynching.

When the dispatcher sent us toward Bryant School at 11:45 PM on New Year's Eve, and we saw the kids running, we figured it was the Beliefs.

Butras heard "Bryant School" and said, "Let's leave 'em alone tonight. It's New Year's Eve. Let them kill themselves. Who gives a fuck?"

•

WALKING the Pompan streets in my uniform those first nights made me feel that every thought of mine, every part of my body, was banging against another thought, another body part. Sometimes I took out my pen and pad and took notes on the events of the day. My mind worked hard in the cold air. I wondered if people looking at me could tell I'd only been a policeman for a few weeks, that I wasn't really experienced. It was all a game, and I could play it as well as any other guy. I wasn't afraid.

I'd never spent so much time outside at night before. Slow chill, blue haze. Too tired to lean against buildings, afraid to stop moving. I would relax by thinking of Clarise, all her moods, the details of our first dates, what she wore. I tried to remember the feel of her forearms and wrists, pulling back her sleeve and tracing the tendons with my fingers. The nervous glitter of her eyes were the streetlights on windows.

At odd moments I enjoyed the danger of it, the shadows, and not knowing what was real. But mostly it was a slow game, and it struck me as strange that I should be doing this at all. I worried that I wouldn't be aware when I needed to be, so I forced myself to study each street, every intersection. I imagined people hiding. I imagined that I was a ghost sliding down the street and I could see them. Music that I'd heard that day hummed inside my ghost head. Sometimes I was hypnotized by the shadows and the changing lights against the gray sky.

Sometimes I'd try to put on this mean look. A grown-up version of the look all the back-hatted little kids had.

•

ON Tuesday the 9th at 6 PM, the dispatcher sent us to 205 Pinehurst Avenue. We arrived before the ambulance.

A man about my father's age—who looked like my father, but brick-brown and with more gray on top—answered the door. He led us into the den where he had found his wife on the floor when he got back from work, her blueberry muffin half-eaten, the television on. His upper lip was perspiring and he held onto the green curtain when Butras crouched to check if she had a pulse. The air in the room smelled stale. There were tulips on the table, still unwrapped, that he'd come home with.

When the EMTs arrived, Butras put his hand around the man's shoulder and took him out of the den. In the kitchen, I heard him tell the man that because his wife had died unexpectedly, an autopsy was needed.

"Is there anybody I can call for you?" Butras asked.

The man sat heavily as we heard the paramedics work behind us.

"Can I get you a drink of water?" Butras asked.

I wondered how many times Butras had done this; I wondered how many times Clarise would do it.

"Could I have my wife's ring?" the man asked.

Butras nodded and went to the sink and took a bar of soap and then he left me and the man in the kitchen. I didn't know what to say so I looked over my shoulder at Butras in the den rubbing the soap on the dead woman's finger until the ring slipped off. He brought it in to the man as her body was taken out.

•

I was surprised that my father invited me to swim with him at the YMCA. He swam a mile every morning.

I was there on Wednesday the 10th at 6 A.M., although I'd gone to bed just four hours earlier after a quiet night in the car. The pool was newly opened, the water without a ripple. My father went to work in the city before rush hour and had to get in the water early. I hadn't seen my father undressed in years. He still had big shoulders and a big chest. Somehow I would have thought my father had shrunk a little. At sixty-one years old he wasn't a fast swimmer but he could go far; he did forty minutes without a break in his big, old floppy blue boxer swimsuit.

In the past, if I made it fifteen minutes in the water, I was lucky. I started looking at the clock, thinking about getting out. After eleven minutes, I began to feel as if I were sinking. The water made me tired when it was cold, which it usually was. At the end of fifteen minutes, I was always exhausted. My arms went first, heavy and achy; then my butt. It was a breathing problem, I decided. Not breathing out enough when my face was down; not taking in enough air between strokes.

My father gave me some tips. Try breathing on your left *and* your right. Don't go so fast at first, ease into it. He had plenty of new ideas for how I could last longer. Maybe that was why I went with him only once in December.

There was a pleasure in going that morning though I had arrived wary of my father. No one around but men at that hour. Men with little blue bubbles over their eyes. Everything tinted blue. Slimy tiles and the thin smell of bleach.

I liked the sauna after the pool. We talked about his legal cases, we talked about the family, uncles and aunts and dreamy unemployed cousins. We talked about the Knicks and Ewing's bad knees. We talked about how good it was of this YMCA to have a sauna. My father was in a good mood. We had the place to ourselves. My nose tingled from the thick eucalyptus scent. It was hard to look my father in the eye sometimes. I had grown up diverting my eyes as a sign of respect. When I asked his opinion of the lynching, he was relaxed, sweating heavily into his towel, big fingers spread over his knees.

He said, "The law doesn't work when the police don't want it to, and my sense is the police didn't try real hard after the cameras went away, after the media got bored. The mood's changed around here. People talk now about the "direction" of the town. Shop owners aren't like they used to be. Pompan was never an over-friendly place, but it wasn't unwelcoming."

"Maybe it's been that way for a long time and you just realized."

"I've always been pleased with our decision to live here," he said.

After he left for work, I stayed on in the Y's weight room which was empty except for the machines and the mirrors. When I worked out alone, I felt clumsy and there was none of the performing, the rivalry, that I was used to. Sometimes I used that emptiness to make me angry, to make me work harder. "In perseverance lies strength," my father used to say. I have no motto for my life; my father had enough for both of us.

My life in Pompan was lonely. As I pushed, I screamed out in frustration at the blank walls. I'm a different person in the gym, my body on fire, rigid, my nose filled with my own sweet odor. I crashed through the weights. My muscles locked and unlocked. I thought about Clarise and how remote she was sometimes. My fists clenched, my arms curled, my legs pushed. Forces took possession of me. I liked the heat, my sweat overflowing. I tried to crush the weights, annihilate them. At the end, I felt dizzy from exhaustion.

As I drove back to my apartment, I was thinking about how I still cared about the way my father had treated me long ago. I felt as if some part of me, maybe my secretiveness, maybe my narrow, careful view of success, maybe my problems with Clarise, was due to my father's treatment when I was fifteen. I wondered if he remembered what happened as clearly as I did.

I suddenly remembered Butras from high school. I was a freshman when he was a senior. He was county champ at 156 pounds. A wrestler. A wrestler's mocking walk, a walk that meant contempt, that he could fight. I remembered Butras as a teenage wrestler, as a blonde, five-foot-seven-inch boy who wasn't ever going to grow any more, neatly dressed with no acne and perfect teeth, always looking a little tanned, dark skin, a serious face, alongside Gwen, tall thin Gwen, fine beautiful Gwen. White boy's dream. Everyone knew she was beautiful, even the people who didn't like her, and there were only a few of them. She laughed when Butras laughed, in the halls, outside class, but you weren't sure how much she liked him. You had the sense that she knew this was just for high school and that she would leave him for college and law school. She must have sensed some weakness in him despite his walk.

I never said a word to Butras back then. We were three years apart and lived only a few blocks away from each other. I never spoke with Gwen either.

●

WHEN I got out of the car in front of Bryant School at 11:50 on New Year's Eve I thought: I can't do this. I can't handle this. What made you think you could handle this?

A voice in my head said, Watch carefully. Do nothing. This will take care of itself. The person in front of you will run. This person will run and be gone. This is nothing. You will handle it. Stay still.

The kid stepped out near the edge of the light.

My gun was up and I shouted, "Police."

It was insane to take this job. What made me think I could do it?

I'm sure I shouted, "Don't move. Keep your hands where we can see them."

I aimed at the wall, between the shadow and the light, and I knew I must show no fear.

●

BOTH of us would have admitted that it had been a bad start. Sometimes during those first weeks of December just getting into the squad car together led to disagreement. The tension was like a physical property; we pulled it back and forth. When we could, we stayed out of the car, patrolling by foot, on opposite sides of the street.

We walked our district past the white brick mansions on Lloyd that looked like convents with their circular drives and canvas-covered shrubs. As a boy I had summer jobs mowing lawns on Lloyd. Back then, if I walked in the all-white neighborhood chances were I was going to be stopped. I knew the drill. Cop would ask where I was going. I'd give him the name of the family who hired me. Cop would ask me the address. I'd give it. As a parting shot he'd say, "Don't be out here too late." I got the message.

Butras and I passed the bungalows on Taber with their dog-run wire fences and Virgin Mary statuettes, past the hospital where you could always hear weeping and see the plain silver crucifix hung over the electric Emergency room doors like a dagger about to fall, under the highway where the sidewalk was white from bird shit and the cars overhead wailed around the curve that sent them heading north past our old high school on the right, massive and gray-faced.

I remember the date exactly, December the 11th, when Butras asked at four-thirty in the afternoon, "You like donuts or not?"

"Middle of the road."

"I take Boston Creme, just in case you're buying."

"Got it."

"You like women who shut their eyes or ones who don't?"

"Both," I said.

"You like music. Ever been to an opera?"

"No."

"Ever want to go?"

"Not even once."

"How come you're so clean and scrubbed? You look like everyone's favorite baby sitter. You ought to work for some quiet law firm, smoke a pipe."

I couldn't tell what Butras wanted. But he had never asked me anything personal before, if that was what he was doing. "My father's a lawyer," I told him.

"And you're police? Is your head screwed on right? My dad's retired. A retired investigator."

"A cop too."

"No. He worked for Aetna. Insurance fraud. You know, like a guy disappears on the Jersey shore and no body appears. My father goes out to find the body. Sometimes he also worked as a bodyguard for the president of the company, for extra cash and what have you."

"Oh yeah?"

"Worked right here. Grew up here too in the good old days of Pompan. He knew everybody and everybody knew him. Hurt his back, had surgery, retired. Now he's a track and field judge. Got a certificate. Starts local races, judges tight finishes. Says it's relaxing."

"You mean you don't consider these the good old days?" I asked.

"Let's get things straight. Out in the open, OK. Issue One: What do you think of welfare? You for or against?"

That was like Butras, changing the conversation, pushing at me. Turning the tension up a little. I never knew which way things were going.

He didn't give me a chance to answer.

"I look at it like this," he said. "I got a friend who works probation in the city. 'Were criminals, always will be criminals,' he says. Don't want jobs. Don't want them. His people say: a two week vacation? Nine to five? Gotta come in everyday? Naah. Not for me, that kind of work. It's a calculated business decision. Don't mind going to jail if I live the way I want the rest of the time. That's how they think. Get their welfare. So they decide their job is to rip people off. Fuck 'em. If they want Reeboks, let them go get a job."

All of a sudden, he was screaming. I didn't know what to make of Butras' anger. Was it even anger?

"Forget it! You and my father are interested in this lynching, the two of you," he said.

"I ought to talk to him about it. Why's he so interested?"

"You're not talking to my father and my father's not talking to you."

I left it alone.

•

WHEN I called Cedric, I went on about Butras as usual. Cedric said, "The guy's talking codes, that's all. You got to read the codes."

Cedric said some wonderful things and some ugly things, but to me he was energy. He was all focused. He examined everything his own way, and there was always drama. He told me better stories than I ever read in the paper. I don't know where he got them. "You ought to write your own personal newspaper," I used to tell him.

Christmas three years before, I brought Cedric home and my mother asked me, "He's not going to curse in front of your father, is he?" She'd heard my stories. "Because he'll be thrown right out of this house."

"No, he's not," I told her. "Don't worry about that. It's just hard for him not to. You know. But he understands it's not cool to say his things today."

Cedric was generally on good behavior with my parents.

On the phone he told me, "Your partner's talking code. You are hearing the fears of white America. You are hearing the fears. You're a policeman now, my man. That means pretty soon you're also gonna understand that violence is neither right nor wrong. It's just a question of who has the power. It's not right or wrong to kill. Killing goes on.

"Fourth time in a year, last week, that police killed an unarmed black man on the street. Never seems to happen the other way around, does it? A white man minding his own business ends up dead from the police.

"Only some weird cases where white men end up dead. Like your lynched man. A white man who didn't like him killed that hanging man," Cedric speculated. He'd held to that theory since the first day we put the picture on our refrigerator.

"For what reason?" I asked.

"Practicing."

●

POLICE work took us to odd places—graveyards, hospitals, inside peoples' homes, restaurant kitchens—it was an endless adjustment to different surroundings. It was mostly car work, though. On Saturday night the 13th, we got gym duty, keeping control of the basketball game at Pompan High. There'd been some fights between rowdy fans from opposing schools the last few games and the school had called us in. We made sure beers weren't smuggled in, made sure no fights got started.

At the game, I felt nostalgic, and in disguise. I was only five years older than the seniors, but there was now a barrier between us, with me in my uniform. They looked at me hard, trying to understand how I had come to be in that uniform. They had no idea.

It was the first time I'd been back at the gym: tight bleachers that pulled out and always seemed to be slipping back and about to crush someone, the too-hot lights, sweat smell, the shellacked-wood court, the glass backboards, ceiling bulbs that splashed three rings of light on the playing floor, the ropes you could climb to the ceiling off in a corner, the janitors who stopped working and stood by the rear door watching. When I drank from the water fountain just outside the gym, the water was as warm as it had always been.

As if he had been thinking about it for a long time, Butras said to me, "You went to this school, right? I don't remember you."

"I was three years behind you, I believe," I said.

"That's what someone told me," Butras said.

"Yeah. I didn't like old Pompan High much."

"I wrestled a black guy once. Pretty good wrestler. I think he was on the Rogers team. Know him?" Butras asked.

"What was his name?"

"I can't remember."

"I didn't know anybody over there. You remember your matches, huh?"

"I nearly killed him. I was *trying* to fucking kill him. He was a big mouth."

●

THE light in this white room is always dim. The question I now have time to consider is: Did I participate any more than simply being present at a moment of violence?

Brenda was here today, smilingly tired. My father too, eyes blood-shot. They look away quickly; they can't stand to look straight at me for too long.

I knew when I started on the force that I had to be cautious. There was trouble waiting to rub off on me in my hometown, a town that now claims a lynching to its credit. The lynching, from the beginning, had the feeling of mockery to me, cruelty out of the blue.

Just as my mind returned to the lynching each and every day of December, now, December gone, no matter where my mind wants to go, it returns to the wall of Bryant School. The nearby, fallen-down fence; the empty sidewalk, not a pedestrian to be seen; the wind carrying trash and a turned-out umbrella. I hear myself screaming in pain. I should stop but I can't. A scream that enters my spine and moves down my legs. A scream that has the smell of blood. The whole bloody lamplit scene dwindling away. I overvalue memory.

•

MY father kept a rifle in his bedroom closet when I was growing up. It was issued to him in Vietnam. It stood upright in a long felt pouch, the butt down behind his shoes and the barrel mixed into some suit jackets. When I was a child, my father showed me how to clean it. There was a long, thin pole with a soft end that we used to clean the barrel, a skinny version of what they stuffed cannonballs into cannons with during the Civil War. If you held it away from you and looked down the barrel it was like looking at a movie camera.

In my memory, I have always mixed up the smell of cleaning the rifle with the smell of shining my father's shoes, where I also used a felt rag to rub in the polish.

On the force, I learned quickly that guns were the thing. I hadn't expected that from so many of the men. But they were young men like me, and they really enjoyed taking their guns out, holding them in the station. Few of them had ever come close to firing one, except at the range.

As a cop, the first question you tried to figure out in any situation was who else had a gun. I learned early on: sure you could go ahead and care if a guy had stolen property on him, but you bet your ass you'd care if he was also carrying a gun. Not because he might shoot the next person he robbed, but because he might shoot you.

The first time I held the pistol on the day they gave it to me at the Academy, it felt too short. My hands remembered holding my father's rifle.

Butras was always playing with his pistol in the car as we drove. On

December 15th, when I asked why he always had it out, Butras said, "Grow up, will you?"

Butras told me his story about joining the Pompan police five years earlier, how he hadn't done well in school and tried college for a year, how he was carrying on the family tradition, how he liked being involved in the business of Pompan and had seven commendations to back up his reputation. When he informed his younger brother (who was then only nine years old) that he was becoming a cop, Larry said, "I dare you to arrest me."

"My little brother, Mr. Tough guy," Butras said. "My scrawny little brother thought he knew all about guns. At nine he couldn't even do a pull-up and he knew about guns."

"The gun's a big deal," I said to Butras.

"It's what makes you a cop."

•

WHEN four inches of snow fell in the space of two hours during the early evening of December 16th, something changed between Butras and me. Maybe it was merely that we found out we shared at least one thing: neither of us slept well. Maybe it was the steady blowing outside the car, the extravagance of the weather, that woke us up to each other.

"This happens once a year, snow like this," Butras said. "What time do you get up in the morning?"

"I get up at three and five and I get up for good around seven."

"What do you mean three and five?"

"I wake up during the night. That's all."

"Me too. One and five. I oughtta call you."

"I'm home."

"You watch CNN?"

"If I can't get back."

"I usually try to catch a little news while I'm up. I watched the whole Gulf war in the middle of the night. I saw all the fireworks before anyone else."

My waking at night drove Clarise crazy. She liked her eight hours; she was a late riser. She thought I actually liked getting up at night. But the next day my sleeplessness sometimes made me feel aimless and a little sad. In the morning, I craved sleep. I was tired most days, although after years of this schedule, I'd grown used to it.

Butras said to me, "Soon enough you'll know that when you're in uniform, you're an asshole to everyone."

"That happens?" But I knew he was right. When a couple of kids came up and asked me a question, the moment they left they were talking about me. Just like Butras had said would happen.

"You'll see," Butras said.

"Maybe it's just you."

"If I did something that needed to be done, I don't mind being an asshole," Butras said. "What I mind is that they can call you an asshole and you still have to smile."

It was a small town and some people came up to say hello and I didn't know who they were. I thought that I'd find nearly all my work comfortable, but it hadn't turned out that way. Because Pompan was small, it didn't take long to feel as if I couldn't find a place to relax, other than inside the car. Walking the street, people just came up to us, asking directions, asking about robberies in their neighborhood, reporting suspicious activity. To escape, I even drank my coffee in the car, and I felt bad about it sometimes.

•

AT the beginning of every shift, Butras picked me up at the station (he often kept the squad car in his driveway during the day) and we picked up Joey Ip at Plasticast where he was coming out at 4:10 from a day's work. Joey was a blind guy who Butras had grown up with. From what I could tell, Joey worked with his hands at the end of a factory line molding plastic and he always smelled like turpentine when he got into the car. Joey hated buses, so Butras picked him up at work and the three of us drove to Bagels Up on Oak Lane where we dropped Joey off. Joey sat behind the screen in the back.

Butras rarely said more than, "Hey, how's it going?"

Joey rarely said more than "Another day, another dime," but it was a ritual for them. I had the sense that Joey just liked being in a police car getting a lift.

That was the start of our shift every week day, Joey getting out at the curb and tapping his way into the bagel shop, getting in line wearing all black like he always did, a crow with dark glasses. Butras would wait until Joey got inside safely, like Joey was an old woman or something. As Butras and I drove off, I'd look over at Joey standing inside the shop, tipped a little to the left, waiting for his sesame seed and his coffee.

•

ON the 17th, we got a radio call at the start of our shift that a man with a gun sticking out of his boot was spotted at Almacs. We put on the lights and got over there quickly. The dispatcher said that the man was about 50 years old and was walking with his hand guiding the elbow of a woman who was approximately his age. They were moving very slowly through the store and had not threatened anyone.

The manager who had called in the complaint, a middle-aged guy with a southern accent in a blue-striped apron, met us at the front door and pointed to the aisle that they were in.

Butras calmly turned down aisle six and walked right up to the man. I was a step behind. The man didn't look twice when he saw us heading toward him. He just continued with his shopping. No one else was in the aisle.

"Excuse me sir, do you have a license for that gun?" Butras asked.

"Who's he?" the man asked Butras, jerking his chin at me. He was about 6 foot 4 inches tall and had long, wet-looking hair that turned yellow over his ears.

"He's my partner," Butras answered.

"A new man, huh?"

"You have a gun in your boot that is exposed and is bothering people in this store," Butras informed him. "Do you have a license for it with you or at home? If not, I will need to confiscate the gun."

"President Clinton is taking all our guns away. He likes your minorities. I'm no fool. Look at the lynching we had not a mile from this spot. That's why I walk my wife everywhere. I believe in my heart it's coming, and I know they'll be a whole bunch of people prepared like I am in case things get bad."

He didn't look at me once. He was a stupid, scared guy and he pissed me off, but Butras was handling it.

"So you have a license," Butras said.

"Sure I do. At my house. That's the law, isn't it?"

"Well if you give me the gun for now, we'll drive over there with you and see what you have."

The man turned to his wife, who was standing behind him. She was a foot shorter than he was and wore red sneakers. "We'll have to shop later. Seems like we have to go home for a bit."

He reached down and handed over the gun to Butras. Butras unloaded the six shots that were in the .25 caliber, and we walked him out of the store to his car. We followed him home to a small apartment at the Western end of Pompan and waited in his living room until he showed us the license.

"Why don't you just leave your gun in your house for the time being," Butras said.

"Why doesn't he?" the man answered, pointing at me.

•

BRYANT School was near The Plaza. The Plaza was three blocks long, had a Sunoco and an Exxon on either end, a hardware store, Mike's barber shop (with its antique, upward-winding, red, white and blue barber pole outside its big glass window), the Imperial Garden for chinese food, Miller's stationery store, The Garden City Bank in clean white sandstone (which was adding a drive-thru), a watch repair place, a liquor store, a dry cleaners, a video rental store called Moviemore, and a Goodwill. The Plaza was really just a collection of stores; no one really lived around it. The neighborhoods started uphill on the other side of the railroad tracks which ran behind the stores. Lincoln Street ran through Oak Lane and a mile away, through The Plaza, then past a few medical offices and curved down hill leading toward Bryant School which was on the south edge of Pompan near the town line with Willis. Kids from Bryant got candy at Miller's after school, crossing the tracks on their way home.

It was 11:45 PM when the call came in New Year's Eve and we were rolling through The Plaza for the third time, just passing Mike's barber pole, dark and motionless for the night. Four hundred yards ahead, but out of sight on the other side of the medical offices, was Bryant School. We didn't need our siren; there was no one on the road.

It had already been a long night. The last call had been two hours earlier (we listened to other cars get dispatched) directing us to a car parked suspiciously and for too long near the reservoir. We had come up on it from behind without a response. We got out with flashlights and checked in the rear window and found a girl and a guy screwing in the backseat. The poor guy was too excited to talk straight once he got his pants up. Butras called him Valentine.

"Valentine, what are you doing in there?"

"Sorry sir."

"Little cold for that, don't you think Valentine?"

"I think so," I answered for the kid who was too shocked to say much.

Butras told him that such public displays of affection could land him in jail, and Butras told him about birth control: his zipper.

Then he said, "And have a happy New Year."

That was worth a good laugh. Leaving, we both regretted not getting a good look at the girl through the foggy glass. We only made the guy get out and talk to us.

•

BUTRAS was always talking about how he hated teenagers. He had this thing about them. He hated their clothes; he thought they didn't have respect for anything; they ruined buildings with their graffiti.

"Fucking kids have no sense," he said.

I reminded him that he had been a kid not so long before.

"What happened between us and them?" he asked. "I wasn't like that. You probably weren't like that. Something's gone wrong. Values. Where are their fucking values?"

Teenage pranks were the reason for many of our calls, and Butras raged about them. Otherwise, he had good manners.

"We should be public servants, but we should not be subservient." More of his code.

"If you're arrogant or what have you, you won't be any good at police work," he told me. "Arrogance is hard to control. If you understand that, you'll do good work."

Even though it was winter, teenagers were still sitting on benches over by Oak Lane, drinking beer, getting drunk, running around, getting ready to drive their cars up people's lawns a few blocks away when we were gone.

"Why do you always have that smirk on your face?" Butras asked me.

"It's a smile," I said.

"It's a smirk. And I can't tell if you're laughing at me or you're just thinking of something and it's amusing you, or what."

"A lot of people have told me the same thing," I told him. "I can't do anything about it. It's the way I look."

"Now give me a smile so I know what a real smile looks like on you. Go ahead."

I showed my teeth and squeezed open my lips. I felt like a horse whinnying.

"Now that's a smile. The rest is a fucking smirk," Butras said.

"Now what I just gave you was a *fake* smile," I said. "Which I save only for special occasions."

"Officer, you've got to work on this to get anywhere in the world," Butras told me.

Since I was a boy I had been told that I had a difficult face to read. I thought I was smiling and everyone else said I was smirking. It made me look in the mirror a lot when I was a teenager. My natural smile remained small and was a little lopsided, just about half my front teeth showed. My eyebrows moved unevenly. My face was wide like my father's.

When I grew older, I liked that people didn't know what I was thinking because they couldn't read my face. But I also didn't want people to think I was against them, that I was trying to act superior. Only when I was twenty, in college, did I stop worrying about my "smirk." I realized that there was nothing I could do about it and when people got to know me they'd be able to tell my smile from annoyance. I hadn't really thought about it much until Butras brought it up again.

Clarise said my smile made me look "mischievous."

I didn't see her enough.

•

I have to feel the pain when I'm lifting. And if it's going well, I don't hear the guy next to me grunting. I'm in a zone.

I force my attention onto every repetition. Lifting is all in the mind. If I'm not feeling my bicep getting stronger while I'm working it, I force my attention back to the working muscle. If I'm distracted, I remind myself of that day's plan.

On good days, I work my sets and I can't find anything that breaks my attention. Mental intensity is physical intensity. You have to crush the machine, hurt it, and in turn it will hurt you and make you hard. Hard as a shell. I clench myself, clench everything together.

I can bring my muscle size up. I can will my muscles to grow.

I see myself as massive when I'm lifting. I feel like I'm breaking something every second, breaking out.

Cedric brought Clarise here today. Talk is a help for them; any words, it hardly matters. I know Clarise wants to run away when she sees me, but of course she can't. She wants to run from her brother too.

Not knowing what happened, she wants to understand why I was willing to make enemies in the world.

I'll answer her when I have something to say, when I understand, when I have a sense of control again.

•

EACH Saturday morning we had a squad meeting. On December 20th, Butras complained to everyone about his stomach.

On the ride out, he told me, "My fucking stomach is acting up again. I got to quit smoking."

"Save you some bucks," I said. "They say if you do a pack a day and you quit and put that money away for a year, you can buy yourself a new car."

"Fuck it. I don't want to quit smoking."

"So don't."

"Sharpens my memory. Keeps me awake."

"I need something for my memory too," I told him. "I can't remember anyone's face anymore."

"You think we're getting old?"

"Not me. I just can't remember."

"I'm terrible too. Names and faces. Can't blame that on the smoking or what have you."

"If you need to remember something, you will."

"I don't know how I started on these fucking cigarettes."

"Well if your stomach's bad, it's probably a good idea to quit."

"I only smoke eight a day."

"That's probably enough to turn your stomach."

"I guess."

"And you used to call yourself an athlete."

"Fuck you," Butras said. "I can still kick your ass. I guarantee that. Right now. Let's go right now."

For a moment, Butras reminded me of Cedric.

•

I could see in front of the car the only one remaining, and he was wearing a dark wool cap. The kid turned and the floodlight reflected off the zipper on his open parka. I saw his hands going for his pocket. I felt my own hands move, almost imitating the kid's hands, as if we were sharing some secret signal.

Not once, in the month we'd been together, had I removed my gun during the hours of our shift. I had been to the practice range a few times; you had to go twice a month. But mostly it sat in its leather pouch weighing on my right hip. The first week it had made me feel uneven. I touched it often in an absent-minded way.

I called out to the kid and then, with no warning, there was white smoke in the black night, smoke coming off the end of my body where my hand was, like I was tossing talc on myself as I did every morning after my shower, before my boxers and the blue uniform went on.

Then I couldn't move my feet, my heavy feet. Shiny black shoe feet.

I could hear Butras running off to my left, a scuffing sound on the pavement. Butras ran low. Butras was in a race, he was moving toward the lights, the victory lights twenty yards away.

It was pitch-black and I was squinting. The bright lights from our car made the sidewalk in front of me like a ball field. The cap made the kid's head round as a ball. I was seeing things. I was hearing voices.

I was standing, legs apart, like I was about to dive into a pool. Like it was a race, and the gun went off, and I couldn't lift my feet, couldn't get into the air and over the water. On the starter's block with shiny black shoes on my feet. I would have to climb down off the block and head home and let the others swim the race. But I couldn't get down off the block either.

When I pulled the trigger, I was astonished that the gun fired. There was no warning. I didn't believe it even when my hand popped back. It was all invisible except for the white smoke. I didn't remember lifting my arm or extending it.

I heard, after I shot, and just before he started to run, Butras yelling out from where he was off to the left, "What the hell was that?"

On the edge of the darkness was a shaft of light filled with a shadow that had fallen into it and seemed to be moving. The body on the ground on its belly had a rhythm. The kid was dancing in a jangling way. The black wool cap was rubbing the pavement, it couldn't get off the pavement.

I thought for a moment that I was looking out a window watching all this as I had once sat in our Pleasant Street house near Rutgers, looking out the kitchen window and watching the neighborhood kids play in the ragged oaks, crash bicycles, rush to make curfews. I thought I was inside a house and the kid on the ground in front of me was outside, far away.

It seemed hours before that we had gotten out of the squad car in front of Bryant School. I heard a bottle rolling down the street and felt some wind. I heard sirens.

The hot white smoke was going up over my head and my gun was hanging down like some long black root that I couldn't pull up. And Butras was scuffing, full speed and low, over to the kid.

Butras moved as if he were drunk, in a curving line toward the kid on the ground; he wanted to set a difficult target as we'd been taught. He moved in a crouch, a few steps left and few steps forward and right, as if he were in a war movie, on patrol. But his shoes were loud. Anyone could hear them. They were louder than what the kid's shoes had sounded like.

There had been other times I had this spying feeling, the feeling of watching from an undeclared space where no one could see me. As a boy, I used to wait for my next door neighbor to appear. A crazy woman who was fat one season and skinny the next, who came up some stairs from her basement parting some beads instead of opening a door to feed the birds. A woman who wore shawls and slippers, whose hair hung in unwashed bands. She would walk around the yard, talking to the trees, alone in the world. I spied on her, wanting to see and not wanting to see.

I saw Butras reach the kid. Butras bent low until he was kneeling. Butras stayed like that on his hands and knees; he looked as if he were thinking. Butras touched the kid in a gentle way.

•

WHEN the gun went off, my ears were ringing. I thought I heard Captain Cuvin's voice from that first orientation at the Pompan Station. Cuvin was talking about the role of the Pompan police force in 1999. In the cold of the street, I remembered bits of that introduction:

". . . the growing ineffectiveness of police in the big cities . . ."

". . . the overflow of city garbage to the suburbs . . ."

". . . here in Pompan we make a difference . . ."

". . . keep an open mind but use your common sense . . ."

". . . the risks of action often outweigh the risks of inaction . . ."

I remembered the policeman's prayer that Cuvin gave each of us on a xeroxed page at the end of the hour: PREPARE US FOR ADVENTURE, BUT DO NOT SPARE US THE HAZARDS.

•

THE smoke off the gun was like talc. Clarise taught me about talcum powder. She called it "ashes." She sang when she splashed it on, "Ashes, ashes, we all go down." She had all these smells in her room from the perfumes she mixed herself. She always smelled good.

The braid of smoke was rising up in front of my eyes, and in the cold night I began to see things through it: Clarise, the first time we did the wild thing up in her third floor room, the white light pouring in through the skylight over the bed, blinding us, our bodies twisted in the black sheets which circled us like a nest, my eyes closed or open, unable to see anything when they were open, at noon, at lunch time, the sun directly overhead through the slightly open skylight, bouncing off the white walls I'd helped her paint, Clarise, dark and warm and wet beside me, on top of me, under me, a moving, open mouth, a thousand mouths, and I was helpless and always near the edge of the bed almost falling off, before she would pull me back with her strong legs.

●

THE pistol kicked like a car backfiring. There was a powerful, dry smell. A lit smell. A thousand matches struck at once, inches from my nose.

My hand was roaring.

The explosion was like the great storm of a human voice.

After the noise was a silence.

In the echo of the shot, I closed my eyes. I felt very sleepy. Almost immediately, Cedric loomed before me, scolding, but I couldn't understand the words. We were in some enormous, dark room. A room with black curtains, maybe a theatre. There were spot-lights. Cedric came up to me, his face darkening, his fists up, ready to fight.

Then I had the sense that I was rising, levitating, like an actor in a play being pulled up above the stage by strings. I was staring down at my stiff self and the fallen body in the light twenty yards away. Yet in the air, I relaxed.

And up there with me was Clarise, going down on me. Both of us up in the air, floating, and she was going down on me with an ice cube in her mouth.

I was shivering. And I was screaming.

•

PART TWO
))((

BUTRAS bent low and gently touched the kid. Then he stood and threw his radio against the wall of Bryant School. He bent again and took something from the kid who was still squirming on the pavement. And then Butras was back beside me screaming into my face, his teeth sharp.

"You stupid, fucking nigger. What the fuck did you do?"

That's where I guessed the story between me and Butras would end. There was no other way. We responded to a gun call and we got there and I thought this kid was drawing a weapon and I pulled the trigger and I will never be right again, our lives will never be the same. I knew this even without knowing another thing about the body on the ground, half in the shadow, half in the light.

Now I can talk plainly about all that happened.

I am already past my time with Frank Butras.

I sing to myself in this white room—half song, half prayer. In the tapping of the radiator I hear the hard blows of my mother's funeral—shovel stabs, door slams. I feel the momentum of tears.

I have never minded being alone, and I have never minded hard work, but when the 8PM nurse leaves I am alone and work to remember the details of New Year's Eve. My memory has had practice. There can be nothing like this bed to bring self-awareness and clarity. The angel of reality visits here. Each moment stands out in my mind, and I take for granted that I need to see each moment again so that some day I can remember a time when I did not yet know about being a policeman.

If I chose to speak I would repeat the words my father said each morning to my sister and mother and me as he came into our sleepy kitchen in Pompan for his bowl of cold fruit, "It's a great day to be alive."

But I keep silent. If anyone knew I could speak, the questions would begin and never end.

I am now wise enough to know that there are actions which can only be explained in part, even in hindsight. Looking back after everything, my decision to return to Pompan—a place that at one time I'd been sure I would never revisit—makes perfect sense to me. I knew many people, people who would help me in my new job. Yet soon after I arrived, I found that places I'd been to hundreds of times as a boy left me shaking my head in wonder. The people I met were not as I remembered. In Pompan, there was the familiar, but also a strangeness.

I am not bad and I am not dangerous and I have brought this trouble on myself. My story is not that simple and I won't, even in the months ahead, give in to such a self-destructive formula. That's too familiar a tale for young black men like me.

I've tried to see the truth about myself. I will answer only for myself when the time comes. And I will lash out at convenient theories about people who are too easy for me to judge, and hope that these people will resist judging me as well. The scenes I flash back to, scenes in which I played a part and are like burrs caught in my memory, are easier to consider after so many visits to them. But in my position, it is not hard to keep secrets.

•

I saw the news conference on television from this hospital bed New Year's Day. Captain Cuvin, as formal as I ever saw him, with a blue cap afloat on his white hair, in front of the cameras:

> Officers Frank Butras and Donald Gambell responded to a call from the Bryant School area this evening. As you are aware, there has been a rise in robberies and assaults in certain areas of Pompan and surrounding communities over the past year. The Department has increased its patrols to ensure the public safety in this area. These officers were patrolling in their squad car when they pursued from the corner of Cedar and Hillside, a group of perhaps twenty or twenty five teens. In front of Bryant school, the two officers got out of their vehicle to pursue the assailants on foot. There was gunfire. The victims were taken to Holy Word Hospital. There is no word yet from the hospital as to the conditions of the victims.

The lieutenant didn't give those reporters the whole story. But they knew there was more and they started scratching around as I would have. They came for me, the jackals.

There I was, on the local news, the photograph from November's story in *The Record*.

When the lieutenant was done speaking, I thought of how, before coming home, I'd always expected life to continue as it was, but with enough possibilities open that when I decided on one, I could develop it in my own way. As I had learned from my father who taught that all things are possible.

I look down at my hands and see them shaking. Beyond my hands, at the end of my hospital bed, I see my father, whom I hadn't expected to see. I've spent far more time with him than I thought I would, and I have forgiven him in certain ways, or at least adjusted my feelings of resentment.

My father always counted on things turning out in his favor in the end, but I wonder how that is going to happen for me.

•

IN my sophomore year of college, I went to a party at a girl's house off campus. It was spring with a just a few buds on the trees, and I had the feeling the mud on the ground could still freeze over-night. The house was about a half mile out of town and three seniors were sharing it. There were bikes lying on the neighbors' lawns and at dusk when we got there, we heard dishes clinking. The place was a typical student house with a peeling yellow linoleum floor in the kitchen and a dish-washer that leaked, leaving a gray puddle sitting in front of it. The kitchen was the only room I saw; everyone was in there cooking chili and eating cornbread out of flat tin pans.

I sat on a bench in the kitchen and a girl sat down next to me. It was Clarise, who lived there.

"How much you think this meal's worth?" she asked.

I looked at her and smiled, a little confused. She had the scent of baby powder and she was wearing a blue leather skirt. She had a dimple in her chin and fine ankles.

"'Cause you're not leaving till you pay."

I picked up on it. "I'm not gonna pay if I gotta sit next to you to eat it."

"You have *never* been so lucky in your life," she said.

That was Clarise. I liked her from that first minute. We went out for the first time that next weekend.

The next year I started tracking her. For almost a year, I followed her without her knowing it. I'd meet her for lunch and we'd say goodbye and go off to different classes and I'd double back to see if she really went where she said she was going, or if she was meeting some other guy. I'd watch her go into her class and fifty minutes later come out and talk to friends, or walk with them back to her house. If I saw her talking to a man, saw her flirting, saw her tongue teasing out at him, I'd just register it in my brain, although I wanted to jump out and fuck the guy up. While there has always been some impulse in me to erupt, there's been another impulse telling me to hide.

I'd call her that night and ask what she'd done that afternoon, who she'd seen, knowing full well what she'd been up to. But I wanted to hear her say it to see if she was telling me the truth. If she told me when she was going out with friends, I'd follow them to see if there was another man. I'd sit behind them at movies; I would check where they had dinner.

She was always honest, but I tracked her anyway.

Cedric knew about my following her and said it was dangerous, said I was going to lose her because of it. But I wasn't going to lose her.

She would disappear for weeks at a time without telling me. I didn't know about Carl yet. I stopped following her after I listened to her speak to the "authorities" about Carl—to the Chicago police, a hospital nurse, a social worker— "There's nothing more I can do from New Jersey. He's *gonna* be in trouble.

"He thought he was Jesus last Christmas too.

"Yeah, he told me he did that."

Her face stiff and awkward, she sat in her living room on a big-pillowed couch plenty of nights dealing with her brother's illness.

•

THE nausea came up so fast under my tongue it pushed me backward. Or was it the buck of the gun I had fired more than once?

I just kept squeezing. I kept shooting and shooting until everything in the clip was gone. Everything in me was gone. I was cold. How crazy I'd gone with a gun in my hand.

I was trying to make myself think clearly. My body was tensed and I could hear myself breathing loudly.

I was the one. I was the one who shot a kid in the dark.

How did it feel for the kid? Had my bullets lifted him into the air before he fell? Had he just buckled over? My thoughts seemed logical but detached.

Far off, I heard the breathing of traffic. The sky was a flat gray like a sky seen in water. Where had I hit him? How bad?

It was a mistake. I was a policeman-in-training, in my first month, and mistakes might be expected.

When my first bullet went off into New Year's Eve, it was like a brilliant messenger.

For a second I remembered seeing Snoop Doggy Dogg on MTV in an interview, how he made a little motion with his hand, how he said, "That's all. Boom." And the interview was over, the screen jumping to some lollipop yellow color.

I felt something like a shudder. I knew immediately, instinctively, that I could only live with the knowledge of having done something horrible by refusing to live with it. It seemed like I was in front of Bryant School, but I was in some unreal world.

I would go and see what I had done and get the kid to Holy Word hospital.

•

I spoke with Cedric nearly every night on the phone during December. Mostly about Butras and sports.

"You see the Knicks last night?"

"Knicks couldn't beat Nigeria," Cedric said. "Remember that skinny seven-six dude Barkely took out in the '92 Olympics? Bam! Elbow in your chest, skinny African motherfucker. He'd never been hit like that in the African Basketball Association."

"I was surprised he didn't quit right then."

"Then Barkely started talking to him."

"Probably making fun on his shoes."

"He was probably wearing old converse All-Stars."

"Remember those?"

"Duck shoes."

"You'd be wearing them if Michael Jordan was."

"Fucking baseball. Thought he could do baseball too. Can you believe that guy."

"He's retired and he's still taking Nike's money."

"Just do it."

"I hate that, man," Cedric said. "Nike Ghetto talk. Racist scam. It's like: Just steal it."

"Knicks have been fucking up."

"They need a guard, or two guards."

"They need the Pacers to have themselves a big, fiery plane accident. Can't even beat Indiana. How they gonnna beat the Western teams?"

•

THE kid was down. There was the sound of gray wind, a rushing, a filling. I smelled the sewage smell we sometimes had coming over from New York or up from southern Jersey. My brain flashed. I heard a bottle rolling and some final, dry leaves. The wind came and spoke with its stink.

Everything was one color as I looked at the box of light the kid lay half in, half out. Everything was gray: pavement, school windows, doorways, trees, clothes.

Ice T singing in my head:

> Violent? You could call me that.
> You think I'm crazy? You ain't seen shit yet.

The kid was down, a shadow letting out blood. Head, round in its stocking hat. The kid was dead for sure and there was nothing between me and the room of bright light that the body lay in, there was nothing between me and the child, and I felt weak and helpless.

Bryant School had cut-out paper snowflakes in the windows of the second floor. Leftover Halloween stuff from two months earlier on the first floor: gravestones, flying witches, ghosts, pumpkins.

Just before I shot, I had been gripping the butt of my gun so hard that the metal digging into my skin left parallel lines on my palm.

My hands were cold and the gun felt warm before I fired; I was cold without my jacket, but my palm was sweating.

The gun stuck to me.

I heard myself praying. I had stopped going to church when I was fourteen. I went twice after I heard my mother had breast cancer. In the cold night air I heard myself say, "Dear God, help me."

"Dear God, I need you."

●

WOUNDED, but they could save him, I thought.

Like Michael Green in high school. He had tried to jump a train one night and missed. His foot got caught under the train wheel and was sliced off. They took care of him at Holy Word hospital.

I hadn't visited Michael in the hospital even though I'd known him all my life, living around the corner from him. I kept trying to imagine Michael and his foot separated: Michael, foot. Had he seen it lying there next to him? Was it knocked twenty feet down the track like you always heard about with train accidents? Where exactly had it been cut off, and would he even have an ankle left on that side? Had he seen his own blood, had he lain in it, or was he immediately in shock, unaware of what had happened?

I collected details from other people who saw him. He was the talk of the school. Our class was undecided whether he was stupid or just unlucky. It was actually sort of cool to hear that he'd been taking night rides on the trains for months. Hanging out in another state then hopping a ride back.

When I thought of him in his hospital room I was overwhelmed by pity. He'd never run again. People would always be staring at his feet, or at the fake foot he'd have to wear in place of the one that was gone.

After a week or so, most of the students had turned on him, had lost their pity. They figured he deserved to lose his leg for reasons that were never exactly clear.

•

BUTRAS had been in a good mood, the holiday spirit. There were private parties happening all around town and he was doing some overtime, working weekend afternoons. People would call in to inform the station about their parties and if over a hundred guests were expected, they'd have to have their street closed down for a few hours. Once police barricades were up, someone needed to be there, to direct traffic and control the scene, and the party-givers would have to pay the overtime bill. Butras took as much overtime as he could.

He had worked a party on Sunday the 21st, the last night that I was with Clarise,

"How was it yesterday?" I asked him when our shift started on the 22nd.

"A wedding. A guy I used to know, Bruce Jansen. I like crowds, you know."

"You've said that."

"The Jansens have some money over there on Forrest Avenue. That's one huge house." He was always impressed by people who had money and made a big show spending it.

"Oh yeah?"

"A hot romance. Bride and groom only knew each other 4 months."

"Won't last," I said.

"When you have money, things last."

"Everyone coming up, saying hello to me. Offering me drinks. Hard to refuse standing out there in the cold. But you got to turn them all down."

"How late did it go?"

"About 1 A.M. They left in a limousine. The whole town watching them get married and I'm watching the whole town."

"How much you make?"

"Three bills, counting tips."

•

EVERYONE always looks at cops and wonders about them. Just like everyone always looks at stewardesses and wonders about them. Maybe it's the blue uniforms. A stewardess in navy blue walks by and every set of eyes moves with her, men and women, wondering: does she want our eyes to follow her? Is that why she took the job? If she wants our eyes, what else does she want? She *has* to know that we are watching.

The same with cops. The uniform attracts attention. Everything hanging down outside the clothes, overloaded, weapons apparent.

But now I know that it's a strange and haunting paradox: certain we know them, without knowing them at all.

•

MY sister never really left Pompan. She even went to college here, Kerr College, over in the brick towers by the river, the huge bronze abstract sculpture at the front gate, enough foreign students to have a first-rate soccer team for a small school. Brenda immersed herself in the landscape of Pompan. When she was not working at the school department, she stayed in and cooked, and ate. Her apartment always had a smell of food.

Pompan was full of women like her, it seemed; she had plenty of friends. Brenda was a big woman with tiny, shrewd eyes. She had hunched shoulders and a bad temper. She liked small men. When she first met Cedric, she asked if he had a girl.

When I told Cedric about her interest, he said, "I don't need *that* much womanly warmth. What am I going to do with a woman bigger than I am, wrestle her?"

My father never needed anything from anybody, as far as I could tell. That's why it was sad to see my sister circling him. That's why I was sorry to hear she'd broken with her boyfriend Howard. I avoided all invitations to the weekly family dinner. My father and Brenda facing each other over her healthy food. Life in the suburbs. What could they talk about?

On the 23rd, Brenda called to say our father had been spotted "slumming" again. A friend of hers had seen him in her restaurant with his lady friend. My sister spoke to me in a tone of conspiracy, but I really didn't care who our father was dating. I felt detached from my father before this latest call from my sister, and I wondered again why I'd come back to Pompan.

"Can you imagine him dancing with someone else, talking close?" my sister asked me. "Can you imagine some woman laughing at his jokes?"

I knew she wanted to say: Can you imagine a *white* woman laughing at his jokes? But she didn't say it because such words would disrespect him. I knew she was beside herself with anger though.

"Why not?" I answered, trying to make her say he was a weak man, that she was ashamed of him. I was confused by my father's interest in this woman. Maybe he was trying to find someone as different from my mother as possible.

"Because your mother died twelve months ago."

"I know."

"Now's not the time."

"Says who?" I asked. But I knew she was right.

"Says people around Pompan who knew mom. They're talking about him. They're shocked, wondering if he's okay."

"Who's said anything to you?"

"Your old neighbors, the Bings."

"Ethan?" I asked.

"Mr. Bing. You know Ethan was in the hospital for a few days. A breakdown or something."

I didn't know and felt bad that I hadn't talked to him since I'd been back.

I couldn't imagine Brenda talking with the Bings about my father, or talking with them about anything for that matter.

"You should tell Dad that you've heard things. That he's self-destructing," Brenda said.

"I don't think so," I said.

"He'll listen to you," she said.

"Come on, Brenda."

"He *will* listen to you."

"Not interested," I said.

"You know I can't understand what you're doing as a policeman," she finally said.

"There are pleasures," I told her.

"Better be," she said.

When I hung up I tried to list the pleasures to myself. For me it was the hours passed in cars—I'd always liked cars—lulled by the vibration, time for private thoughts. For guys like Butras, it was a world of order and purpose and vigilance, and I was enjoying that view of things too.

•

WE watched people walking their kids home from school. We passed the girls with ponytails and six rings through their ears, boys ignoring their parents. And all the while Butras gave me his philosophies: "Walk and talk, that's our job. If we're good, we'll just insinuate ourselves into trouble and it won't surprise us. We're just collectors, Cage. Collectors of suggestions and complaints."

The man could jabber. You get used to looking at someone who sits next to you so many hours; I thought we were getting along okay. I'd gotten used to his monologues too. I was almost glad I was partnered with someone who wasn't trying to be nice all the time. I knew his tics: The yellow tree vanilla air freshener he kept on the dashboard; the lunch he picked out of his teeth with a toothpick. All along, I thought, I can learn police work from him. But if I got too personal, his wall would go up. Sometimes we'd be driving and I'd remember Tom Prescott in the station, putting on that show for me early in the month, messing around with Butras so I could see what kind of guy he was. Prescott saying to Butras, "You know why I respect you?"

Butras saying, "Why?"

"Because you're a good teacher."

Butras acting dumb, saying, "Really?'

"Yeah."

"What did I ever teach you?"

"How to call it a day and how to drink until you forget about it."

It was all a show, but it stuck in my head that Butras could teach me something.

"Criminals sense fear," Butras told me more than once as we drove. "They smell it like a dog. Even if you have on a uniform, they're trying to sense fear."

●

ON my way out for milk on the 23rd, I passed Larry Butras walking on Jefferson Road. Like his brother he made no concession to the cold, wearing only a black T-shirt.

I rolled down my window. "Not in school today?"

His expression was flat. He shook his head, fished in the pocket of a shirt for a cigarette, found one crushed in a pack and lit it.

"Not today."

"Something keeping you out?"

"I'm going back tomorrow."

He had steady, hostile eyes.

"You need some help? Is there someone over there I can talk to for you?" I was thinking of doing my partner a favor.

"I don't want you helping me. You'll think I *owe* you and I don't owe nobody nothing." Like half the white kids I'd met in Pompan, he talked black.

The more I looked, the more I could see they were brothers by their eyes.

"Who do you think did the lynching?" he shot out suddenly.

"I don't know."

"You don't know?" he sounded like a maniac. "Homeboy like you don't know?"

•

THERE was a moment of ecstasy. The shot. The tangy smell. I had become violent power. There was no denying that the explosion was dazzling. No one was suffering yet; there was just a wild sound. If someone had been looking at me, they probably would have been startled by my face, my distorted features. Head to toe I was trembling. Defense had become offense. I felt fierce and triumphant and lucky in the night.

Then the blood drained from my head. I looked toward the wall and the light and the fallen shadow.

The light killed him, I thought.

•

THERE will be an attorney. Probably a black attorney. They will hire a black attorney to take me down. That's the way they do it these days.

"Officer Gambell, do you believe that you have some homicidal impulse that other people can't even imagine?"

"No sir."

"Perhaps you have impulses that occur to other people, but they manage to stifle them while you can't?"

"No sir."

"Do you believe that people are masters of their own lives?"

"Yes sir."

"Did your victim ever have a weapon pointed at you?" the prosecutor will ask.

"No. He just pivoted and moved toward his pocket."

"But he never got into the pocket, did he? And he really must have pivoted quickly because you shot him in the back."

There will be an attorney who will say I was so angry and frightened that I lost control.

And I will tell him I only did what I had to do in that split second.

●

BEFORE New Year's Eve, I had been to Bryant School once in December. On Wednesday the 24th, I went to show the kids what a black policeman was; they had never met one. I had received department approval for the visit after an invitation from Mrs. Ellis. Her son was in the eighth grade class. The teacher had wanted me to give a talk, but I asked to just come in while the kids were working on an assignment, say hello, get introduced and then just walk among them. It would be more natural that way.

I arrived after lunch. I was wearing my uniform although my shift was three hours away. When I walked into that classroom everything went quiet. They were expecting me. Although they were doing worksheets, the kids stopped and stared at me. All those bright faces were interested for a moment, then wanted to get back to their noisy routine.

I went up to one boy, kneeled beside his desk. I didn't remember the desk being so low.

"What kind of work?" I asked.

"Spelling," the boy mumbled.

"Spelling?"

"Yeah."

"You a good speller?"

"Pretty good."

"Can you spell officer?"

The kid got it right.

"Do you have any questions for me?"

"You ever see a man shot in the head?" the boy asked.

●

WE got a call on Christmas Eve, Wednesday, at around 5:35, that there was a wild animal in a cage spotted on the sixth floor fire escape of the Stanford Apartments. We drove over to the apartments on Greenough Street, toured around the old, white sandstone building once. We passed the green canopy that ran from the front door to the street, and then turned into the driveway that led to the parking lot behind the place. When we got out of the car and looked up the fire escape, we could see the cage but not what was in it.

We entered through the back door and walked to the sixth floor.

On the stairs Butras said, "This one's all yours."

It was the corner apartment. When we knocked, no one answered. I said, "Pompan police," and knocked again and when no one came, I tried the doorknob. It was unlocked.

When I opened the door, three alligators came running at me. They moved fast and low, teeth clicking. I slammed the door and stepped back into Butras' chest.

"What happened?" Butras asked.

"Alligators," I said.

"Fuck you. In there?"

"Check it out," I said. "But I'd go slow, man."

Butras pushed open the door and stuck his head in, then pulled back. "You gotta be kidding."

We went downstairs and found the manager's office, but it was empty so we called back to the station. They thought we were messing around, but we finally got them to call the ASPCA which took forty five minutes to get there.

Two women in black rubber boots and green uniforms carrying long hooked poles walked upstairs with us. They opened the apartment door and when the alligators came running, they poled the animals in the face. It was impressive, like the women had been practicing their alligator flips for years. Butras and I saw their snouts roped up when we got into the apartment.

The place was a jungle: huge ferns, hanging plants, wooden planks stretched between tubs of water, glass tanks. Wandering around the floor were eight iguanas, two more baby alligators—the longest of the captured was three feet—10 turtles, a couple of yellow and blue parrots. It was dark inside, except along one wall where there were two sun-bright tube lights. We were all sweating in the heat.

The cage on the fire escape had a 2-foot gecko in it.

The ASPCA people put the alligators into plastic garbage pails and took them away, but left the rest of the beasts. We brought the cage in off the fire escape.

The neighbors who had come out into the hall to see what was happening gave us the name of the apartment owner. They said he wasn't around much. They said they didn't know a thing about the animals. Back inside the jungle, we left his citation on the fish tank nearest the door.

"The people in this town have gotten crazier since I've been gone," I said to Butras.

"They're fucking nuts," he said.

•

I felt badly about not seeing Clarise on Christmas day. She was at church and I had refused to go with her. I'd been arguing with her about church for years. At Rutgers, she drove to the First Baptist with her friend Gina every Sunday morning. They liked the minister there, Reverend Peeson, who Clarise described as slow-moving. Nearly every Saturday she'd ask me, "You want to come with me tomorrow?"

"It's not my thing," I told her.

"It's a beautiful place." She liked the bells ringing, she liked the singing and the organ and the tambourine playing. When she started going she didn't know a soul, except Gina, but after a while she'd met a few people in the congregation.

"Doesn't mean I don't have faith," I said. "I just can't sit that long. Makes me uncomfortable."

"I don't know. I get solace from the cross," Clarise said.

"You can pray to God without being in a church," I said.

She looked disappointed but defiant. I could never quite put together her wildness and the desire to go to church. It seemed hypocritical to me, in a way.

Some Sunday mornings, I watched her get ready. She wore a long blue dress that was concealing, one that took a long time to put on. She needed my help to zip it. She wore low black heels, and around her neck, a thin gold necklace her mother had given her. She carried a tiny black handbag.

I was sorry that I couldn't go with her, but I couldn't.

"Only the old men go anymore," she said to me. "Maybe you'll go when you're an old man."

"Maybe," I told her.

"You like it, don't you," she said sadly.

"Like what?"

"Your police work."

"No baby. I like being in bed with you."

The day after Christmas Clarise dropped underground again, wouldn't answer the phone. Problems with her brother I assumed.

I was supposed to see her New Year's Day.

•

WHATEVER you did had to be done perfectly; that was my father. This rule applied whether I was making my bed or cleaning my room, or talking to a relative. Sometimes my father would come up from behind and show me how to do it better. He even thought he could crack an egg better. As a boy, if I brought home a 98 on a test he asked, "What happened to the other two points?"

The man grew up in rural Virginia. He was an orphan at age five, raised by an older sister and an aunt Gloria. He started taking pay jobs at eleven.

There was one story he told over and over. It was about a teacher he had in ninth grade. She was a tiny woman with curling arthritis who used crutches to get around. He showed up for a math class unprepared and the lady saw that he had not done his work and called on him to answer problems for the next forty five minutes. He left the room determined never to go back and was walking down the hall when he got tapped on the shoulder by one of the crutches. He was a big guy, a halfback. She came right up close to him, pressed him against a wall and said, looking up into his face, "You think I humiliated you because I wanted to? You humiliated yourself. Don't ever come back to my room without knowing your work. I will help you. Otherwise, get out of here and be a bum."

My father was a serious man, a good thinker. My father had contempt for some people and wasn't good at hiding it.

I never protested in my father's house, not even when I came back as a policeman. There were rules.

•

"THE Butras family knew that lynched man real well," Brenda told me the day after Christmas. She'd been doing some hunting.

"You'll make detective before I will," I told her. "What's the latest?"

"Next door neighbor of theirs gets her hair done where I go. Been asking around for you, you know. Seems that the lynched man and the younger Butras boy were in some bad business together."

"What business is that?"

"The lynched man had been stealing things forever. Then the brother started stealing things with him. Even stealing from the boy's father."

I wondered if the FBI had this information. Were these things brought out into the open when they were in town? I wanted to give Harold a call in Detroit to ask him how to pass on these facts without seeming simple if the FBI knew them already.

"Your partner's father had a soft spot for the lynched man, used him as a fix-it man, knew him when they were in Pompan High School together. Lynched man was like some genius with machines, even though he was drunk half the time. When the father found out that his son was criming with his grade school buddy, he threw the man out, sided with his son. The lynched man and the boy stopped talking around then. A simple case of falling out among thieves."

"So who killed Wilbourne?" I asked her.

"You're the police. Aren't you supposed to tell me it was Wilbourne's son, beaten once too often by his old man? Isn't that the official story? All I know is the lynched man was one nasty piece of work and nobody around seems to care who killed him."

"The unofficial story is that one night when he was picked up drunk, he punched a cop in the face, knocking out some teeth and after that everyone on the force hated him," I told her.

"Those men hate everyone."

•

"YOU married?" Butras asked on the 26th just after we dropped off Joey Ip.

"No. How about you?"

"No. Why are you wearing a silver bracelet on your wrist then?" Butras said what he was thinking, straight out.

Clarise had given it to me. Brought it back from Gambia. A hunter's good luck charm. Butras must never have seen a man wearing a bracelet.

"I just like the way it looks," I told him. "I thought you were married? Didn't I hear that?"

"Used to be."

"When?"

"Didn't last long. A year. After high school. It wasn't much to speak of."

"You see her anymore?"

"Never. She's gone. Gone, goodbye. She never liked my father or my brother or how close we were. Good riddance.

"Hey. Happy Christmas," Butras said. "I remembered this morning that I forgot to tell you that yesterday."

"Merry to you," I answered.

•

"YOU remember Justina?" Cedric asked on the phone that night. Most nights we talked after I came in from my shift at one. I appreciated the chance to unwind with him. He always had something to say. I could just lay back and listen to him go on.

"Of course I remember Justina. Short, real dark, big nails, nice legs, ass like a coffee table with two cups on it."

"You know I used to like her, right?"

"Of course I remember."

"She's marrying a white guy."

"So?"

"So I saw her the other day, she's working downtown, and I told her, 'Why would he be marrying a black girl like you? So you got a college degree. So what?' 'The man loves me,' she says. 'There's no benefit for him marrying you. Why's he even thinking about it?' I say to her. 'You racist asshole,' is what she says to me. Can you believe that?"

"What I can't believe is you saying what you said to her."

"What am I supposed to say?" Cedric asked.

"You're supposed to say Congratulations when someone you know is getting married."

"Fuck that. She's getting herself fucked over."

"Says who? You need some help."

"Why do you want to go through your life wanting to be the first black this, the first black that? Who wants to be worrying about that?"

"Uh-huh."

"It's like Spike's always saying: You got to take care of the brothers first."

"Spike's making television commercials."

"That's just a job for Spike."

"Spike's making some money."

"Spike's just keeping his name public. I'll tell you one thing though. Spike wouldn't be the first black policeman in some white suburb. No, not Spike."

"Fuck Spike. You know how tired I am of hearing about Spike?"

•

As I came into the station to change clothes at my usual 3:30 on Saturday the 27th, I heard some of the guys talking. I had stopped outside the locker room to pour myself a coffee. They were always talking, standing around with their stories, but I'd never heard my name mentioned before. I couldn't make out who was who through the closed door.

"Cage is nothing. He thinks he's a goddamn pistol. He walks around like someone is admiring him. Thinks he'll solve the lynching."

"Good luck on that."

"He's a college boy," someone else said. "What do you expect?"

"He doesn't have any balls. Afraid of some alligators."

"I would have shut that door too and run."

"We all know why he was hired."

"Well he did grow up here."

"No. The worst is he looks straight at you when he talks. As if you cared what he was saying."

I knew that high voice. It was Tommy Price, from Pompan High, a year ahead of me, a red-faced smart-ass. I hadn't seen him much since the beginning of the month when we'd nodded at each other in passing.

I heard Butras say, "You know there's nothing as pathetic as a bunch of guys standing around razzing someone who isn't even present."

"You're awfully sentimental about your new friend," one said.

"The guy's trying to be a cop, and what have you. I'm his teacher. You guys are just assholes. Everyone knows there's a problem between us and them. But do any of you know what to do about it? No. I didn't think so. So shut up."

"Now there's a scary thought, you teaching anyone," Tommy Price said before I strolled in.

The room quieted down fast.

I looked at Tommy. "Your true colors were showing Tommy."

"You son-of-a-bitch, chicken shit, listening outside the door," Tommy said.

"Go ahead," I said. From high school, it came back to me, bad feelings. I felt murder in my fingers.

"There are a lot of names I'd call you if we weren't here," he said.

"Why don't you go on and say them," I said. "Everyone here knows what you're going to say."

Tommy didn't say anything.

Butras tapped my shoulder and said, "Let's go."

I never had the naive idea that anyone on the force would care for me. But I wanted to know what they were thinking so I could know if somebody was planning to bring me down. No class at the Academy prepared me for that part of police work.

I was surprised that Butras defended me. But maybe I shouldn't have been; the man talked about loyalty almost as often as he named the stars for me, leaning out the window when we pulled over at night, talking skyward but loud enough for me to hear, telling me the seasons all the constellations disappeared.

•

MOST nights, if things were quiet, I would drop Butras off at his father's house for an hour and he would have dinner there while I'd get a burger at The Floss. Then I drove back and picked him up. He never invited me in to meet his father. I wondered if the FBI had interviewed him after the lynching.

New Year's Eve at around six Butras asked, "You hungry?"

For the last hour he'd seemed lost in himself and he didn't hear me the few times I tried to talk. The wind blowing through the partition of the cruiser, the open window, and the normal rattles had been the only noises.

Pizza at D'Angelos. He had peppers and I had mushrooms on top; we each had small pies with red sauce. He was in his short sleeves and I kept my coat on. Eating, Butras was always making plans. Meals were for looking ahead. Even if it meant just making a route for the evening tour. Two men, covering 100 square blocks, protecting the lives of maybe four thousand people. For five years he had been working out how to get it done efficiently, appearing to be everywhere at once. I remember that when he was talking I was looking down at my badge, #6391.

"Here's the way to go about it," Butras was saying to me. He had some system of half left turns and half right turns that allowed us to take into account all the one-way streets and dead-ends.

"There's no other reasonable way," he said to me.

And if I disagreed with him, on any subject, he held a grudge. He had a perfect memory for even minor disagreements.

Thinking back, with all our meals together and plans, we never really discussed the risks of our job, or how, if there was danger, we would react as a team. He told me how he had handled threats or fights in the past, but I guess we both assumed that a month wasn't very long and the chance of us having to face something together was pretty small.

Butras and I never really sat at a meal and talked about ourselves. Could I imagine telling him about all the things I hate, about happiness? Is it possible that we could have discussed complex feelings? Could I have talked to him about Clarise? Could I have said to him she had a boom-pow ass—she took a step and her ass took three steps? About Cedric? Could I have told him that America is filled with black men like me who are tired of other people psychologizing us, looking for who we are in our handshakes, our postures, our tones of voice? Would telling him this have made any difference in how we got along?

Who was he? A man in a spotless shirt, with blue eyes, thin lips and sharp teeth.

•

WHEN we got into the car after pizza at D'Angelo's at around 7:00 PM on the 31st, the dispatcher called to say I had a phone call from Buzz.

"I don't know any Buzz," I told the dispatcher.

"What can I tell you," Jerry said, and gave me the phone number. Jerry chain-smoked and I could hear him puffing as he disconnected me.

I went back into D'Angelo's to call.

"This is Larry," Butras' brother said on the phone. "I used the name Buzz 'cause I knew he'd be there. I'm calling to tell you my brother is drinking again and you should have a talk with him. My big-fucking-shot brother."

"Drinking again?"

"My brother's a fucking drunk, if you didn't know, pea-brain. An alcoholic. You want me to say it some other way?"

Then the kid hung up.

I had no idea about my partner's drinking history before the call. It didn't sound right; but then it did. Butras' bad stomach. The Rolaids. Prescott's crack in the station about getting drunk. All the cologne he wore, the vanilla air freshener.

Sure, I was one swift fucking cop. No one had told me and I hadn't seen it.

But then I thought: the kid is fucking with me, making things up to take down his brother. Butras never acted drunk around me, not for a second.

●

We hit the raccoon around 7:30 PM, the pizza taste still sour in our mouths. We were riding up Governor Street and I was thinking about the call from Larry. Governor was unlit except for the porch lights on houses that were 80 or so yards apart, separated by maple trees and set back from the curb. We were going about 30 miles per hour when the thing streaked across the street from right to left, a scrambling shadow. There was a small thump against the wheel on the passenger side and Butras immediately knew he'd hit something.

"Ah, shit," he let out.

We stopped and backed up about five feet and got out of the car, leaving it running. The raccoon was split, and lying on its side along the curb like it had popped off the front wheel and fallen back. It was alive and shimmering with its sharp-looking claws; it was fighting pathetically to escape.

"Shit. This thing's probably got rabies," Butras said.

"What are you gonna do?"

"Only one thing to do. Let's get back in the car."

We walked back to our seats, shut the door, and Butras shifted into drive. He angled the tires about twenty degrees toward the curb and slowly went forward crushing the raccoon's head under the same tire that had knocked him back. The sound was a puffiness, then a silence.

"Put the poor guy out of his misery," he said, backing up again.

He parked, got out and went into the back seat for a pair of heavy gloves and then opened the trunk for a black garbage bag and a shovel. He handed the bag to me and scooped up the dead raccoon, sliding it into the bag. Then he tied the bag away and dumped it into the trunk. I watched him work. He didn't seem drunk; he was acting normal.

I admired how Butras had handled the accident, but he didn't like being complimented. We didn't speak about what happened until an hour later when we got a call from the dispatcher who put the sargeant on.

"I hear you guys killed a dog tonight."

"Word travels fast," Butras said. "But that's wrong. It was a raccoon."

"Well, someone on Governor Street reported that your police car maliciously drove over the head of an animal and killed it. They said it was a dog. An animal lover, I guess. Just wanted you to know."

"Hey thanks," Butras said.

When he signed off, he said to me, "You can't win in this job. Someone's always got a complaint on you. Even being humane to damn raccoons with rabies. You can't win. But you have to keep smiling."

•

IN the eighth grade I took an aptitude test at Bryant School. It was a sunny Saturday morning. Inside, there were long, dark corridors I followed to the test room. There were maybe one hundred kids in the cafeteria with me. We sat on those plastic picnic benches, six of us to a table. They didn't look much different from the kids in my class; I had seen a few around. I knew some of the others who went to the middle school across town. There were framed paintings of old white-haired men high up on the walls all around the yellow room.

I sat in the front, nearest to where they set up a blackboard to keep track of how much time we had left for our answers, and near a bronze bust of a man with a wig that I couldn't take my eyes off. The blackboard was as green as a pool table. I remember the test started at 9 AM. I had brought along two sharp pencils. One of the boys on my bench wrote very hard and the whole table shook.

The proctor came in with a white shirt and a tie. He had a limp and he carried a stack of exams under his arms like a football. The man kept blowing his nose into a red handkerchief all morning during the test. Every half-hour he called out the time in a high voice.

I don't remember how I did on the test, but I remember coming out into the blinding sun and running all the way home with energy I didn't think I had left.

•

THE black attorney prosecuting me will say, "A crime was committed New Year's Eve. Would you agree?"

And I will agree.

"Therefore there must be a criminal. Would you agree?" And I will nod.

"And you, the man with the loaded weapon, the one who fired the gun, are the criminal, the assassin. Not only because of your gun, but because you were wearing blue, because of that color and the responsibility it implied. You *were* wearing blue, were you not?"

He will hate me. He will try to humiliate me.

But I am not an assassin. That term does not cover what I've done.

•

MY sister had worked herself up about my father's dating, but I didn't know how she would proceed against him. For all her concerns, I thought she wouldn't have much influence on him.

She called me three nights in a row after Christmas, to discuss his "adventures."

"I hope he's not planning to spend New Year's Eve with her. I certainly do not want to see her at any of my holiday dinners," Brenda said more than once.

After this third call, I realized that Brenda had no plan other than to watch our father as closely as possible and to complain to me about him. I called her back on the afternoon of the 29th, right after I hung up. I was dressing as we spoke, preparing to meet her at my father's house in an hour. She talked so much, and so fast, I hadn't had a chance to tell her what I'd been thinking.

"Why don't you tell him what you think instead of telling me?" I asked.

"You know he'll say, 'Stay out of this business. It's my business.'"

She liked to imagine that she had some authority over him though she knew that no one did now that our mother was dead.

"Tell him you don't want to meet this woman at our next dinner," I said.

"You know he'll say, 'I'll have who I want to my house for dinner.' And anyway, he doesn't even know that I know about her," Brenda said.

"You ought to stop calling me about all this," I told her. "It's your thing."

"If anyone should try to ruin his affair, it's you," she said. "You never liked him anyway. Why don't you call up his lady friend and tell her a thing or two. Tell her a couple of stories about him, about how he used to whack you until you were raw, how he used to lean out from his chair and catch your hand and squeeze it until you screamed. Have her paged on one of their dates. That's the way to end this foolishness."

"You're evil," I said. "I couldn't do that."

"I'm looking after his interest here," Brenda said.

"And I'm happy to not look after our father at all," I said.

•

IN my uniform, at night, early in the month, I was sometimes afraid walking the streets. I never said this to Frank Butras. I saw things at night: who came home from work late, who slept with their light on. But I also saw myself, my reflection in store windows, my face with its silvery-green outline, and I heard things, and was jumpy and alert. Walking alone at night, I felt that I had lots of time on my hands. I thought of the odd people I met during the day. The heavy lady with chopped-up hair who came toward me on Oak Lane shouting, "Have you confessed to God our Savior?" "Yes I have," I told her, hoping she'd move along. "Prayer, that's the thing," she said before walking past me. The man who fell asleep at the wheel at five in the afternoon and drove his car right through a parked car on Ogden Street. Who got out of his car with his stooped shoulders and bad teeth, bleeding from his hawk nose, asking, "What happened?"

At night the town was closed down. Across the street from Butras somewhere out there in the dark, I felt like a target. And I'd feel sick for a second, then positive again. I had energy and just as suddenly a heaviness. Every window caught the light. I thought of Clarise and felt light-headed with the pleasure and mess of our getting together. Sometimes I walked fast, as if I had somewhere to go.

Late in the month was different from the beginning of December—walking through Oak Lane at night, Butras visible across the street—because I felt no fear. Now I only hoped that no one who knew me would come up to me, that I could stay away from people. And I worried, at these times, that if someone gave me trouble, I'd come on too strong, be too rough. I'd be stubborn and forget that I was a policeman. I'd feel myself pumped up like I was in the gym, a little out of control from all the weights, my skin throbbing. As I walked, I tried to convince myself that not everyone was a criminal. I tried to remind myself that we got called only when people were at their worst. I'd become a typical policeman unknowingly; it had filled me up.

•

I met Brenda and Cedric at my father's house for dinner on the 29th, a night off. I still hadn't been able to reach Clarise since Christmas. Cedric arrived twenty minutes late and when he took off his bulky red coat, his left bicep looked to be about twice the size of his right through his shirtsleeve.

"What happened to your arm?" I asked him.

"I'm out running last night, about 5 o'clock along the park, the way I always go, and this dog takes off after me. He doesn't even bark, he just starts running. So I figure he's going to chase me out of his territory or something, then back off, but he's after me longer than he should be. I'm picking up speed and this fucking Doberman is making up ground on me and I see he's serious or crazy, and I know I'm not going to outrun him for very long, but I keep pushing because I'm trying to get out of his zone. I'm running scared. I'm breathing heavy as a mackerel on a dock. But I hear his little clicking feet behind me coming fast, so I stop—I'm beat, I can't go much further—and he jumps at my chest and I put up my arm to block him and his teeth grab onto my arm. I have this dog hanging from my arm and I can see the blood coming out next to his tooth, running down my arm and the pain is burning me up."

"Oh my God," my sister said.

"I start swatting this dog with my other arm, punching him, trying to get him to let go. And finally he falls off and I go up on top of this parked car. I just run up onto the roof of this Toyota which I'm bending in, but I don't care, and the dog doesn't follow me. He stands there looking at me. Then when he sees that I'm not coming down, he turns around and trots off. Somebody must have seen me and called an ambulance because not a minute later, as I'm stepping down off the roof, an ambulance rolls up and takes me to St. Luke's."

"You're lucky that dog didn't kill you," I said.

"I've never seen anything like that animal. Dog went berserk."

"Then he just walked away."

"I called Clarise from St. Luke's and she came over."

"You did?" I said.

"She got there in ten minutes from wherever she was. Talking all her medical stuff with the doctors taking care of me, cleaning these holes in my arm out."

"She hasn't returned my calls in a few days."

"Get yourself bitten, she'll call you," my sister said. She knew Clarise, but I'd never really told her about the disappearances I lived with.

"How'd she seem?" I asked Cedric.

"She seemed fine. Better mood than I was in. She got a cab and took me home when they were done with me."

Cedric rolled up his sleeve and showed us the gauze wrapping the bandages that ran from his elbow nearly to his shoulder.

Every light in the house was on. We were ready to eat early, around 5:30, hungry from sitting around doing nothing all day but watching college football, the cold dark outside making the house feel huge. Ellington was playing duets with Coltrane in the living room. Brenda was cooking a turkey.

●

THE night of the 31st at 9:30 PM, we found Ethan Bing walking past the closed stores and silent barber poles of the Plaza. He looked tiny against the dark stores, the dark sky. I'd heard from my sister that he had taken to wandering after his mother got sicker, a prolonged seizure affecting her ability to think clearly. Despite the temperature, he was in a string T-shirt and gray sweat pants.

Butras pulled the car up alongside him. Ethan glanced over his shoulders at us, slowed down, then finally stopped when I hooted the siren.

I rolled down my window. "It's me, Cage. Need a lift?" I hadn't talked to him since I'd moved back in town, not even after I'd heard he'd been in the hospital. Brenda said he'd turned strange.

"No," he answered.

"What are you doing out here on New Year's Eve?"

He wouldn't look at me; he was studying his feet.

"I needed to get out."

"No law against that," Butras said. "Although there might be someday."

Ethan said quietly to me, "I just needed some time alone." He sounded apologetic.

I could tell he was hanging on to the shreds of his mother. If she died, he was done. He'd be lost entirely. Then I thought: if he dies, she's done.

"How's your mom?" I asked.

"No good," he said.

I realized that Ethan had an unspoken deal with me and probably everyone who knew him: If you don't ask too much, I'll save you from the sad details of my life.

"What do the doctors say?" I asked.

It seemed strange to be having this conversation out here on the street in the dark. Having stopped walking, he was cold, shuffling his feet, arms across his chest. We could have been in his living room, the big TV up in the corner over his mother's collection of colored glass, his father's brown Barca-lounger waiting for its fat occupant.

"They say she's no good and we should get used to it."

"Does she know?"

"She grabs my hands and hangs on no matter what they say in front of her. They talk about her in front of her."

Ethan didn't look at me and I knew he was scared of his own temper, or feelings.

Butras nudged me. "Let's go."

"We're heading on here," I said. "You sure you don't want a ride?"

He looked at me for the first time.

"I've been reading philosophy, you know?" he said.

"I didn't know," I said.

"Yeah."

"I'll call you," I said. But I knew that I wouldn't.

As we drove off, I saw him start off in the direction he had been going (toward the big American flag I could see over The Plaza buildings), quickly pick up his pace, his arms swinging.

•

I'VE broken up with Clarise so many times and each time I miss her. The way she made me take off my shoes at her apartment door, inviting me in. How she sometimes grew her hair and sculpted it up, all beauteous, and how she'd fall asleep over a book and her head would be flat on one side when she woke up. The way she wore blue scrub pants with a little rope belt and a tight v-neck scrub shirt. "*My* blue uniform," she said, grabbing at me, but at the same time telling me about her biochemistry and her pathology classes.

When I see her at the end of my hospital bed, I'm lonely for her. Some days she shrieks with hurt and flings herself into Cedric. She cries for a few minutes and Cedric pats her hair and just holds her. He tells her he won't be leaving for a while. She finally pulls her face away and wipes her eyes with a wrist and smiles.

"I was trying not to do that," she says.

"I hate hospitals," Cedric answers.

•

THERE was a short stretch of dirt road, running through woods, that connected Ballard Street to Maitland Avenue. It came out in the parking lot behind a small apartment complex. It was about half a mile long and rutted and was really only used as a short-cut between neighborhoods. We had been on it once or twice during the month and we drove it again at around 10:00 PM New Year's Eve. I was thinking again about Larry's call, and whether Butras drank.

I had seen the physical resemblance between Butras and his brother, and this boy was wild, but Butras had somehow been tamed. Maybe it was beer that settled him down.

There was not a white guy I'd ever known who held his liquor well. They were all dangerous once they started serious drinking. But Butras hid it pretty well if what his brother said was true.

Butras and I were both sipping the Cokes that we had picked up at the RediMart on Allens Avenue after the raccoon business.

"I gotta take a piss," I told Butras.

"Don't mind if I do," he said and stopped the car, leaving the headlights on to illuminate the road and the brush and halfway up the trunks of trees in a hazy arc. He got out his side and I got out my side and in the fierce cold, we unzipped and peed right there, each of us aiming our own way.

And while we were busy, Butras said, "Is there anything better than taking a piss outside?"

And I said, "It's too damn cold."

"This is the greatest," he said, speaking to the stars.

I felt this itch on my neck like a fly had landed, and it made me jump a little, flicking my stream toward this small, perfect evergreen that had taken hold just next to the road. In the headlights the tree glistened and bent under the watering. I had picked a place where my piss landed quietly because comparing how long it goes is a guy thing and I didn't want to get into it with Butras and I knew he'd be listening. But when I hit the evergreen there was a little swishing noise and Butras said, "You beat me this time."

He took a long time zipping up and I got back into the car fast and closed the door. Butras' side was still open and he was stretching and shaking his legs out, enjoying the winter air.

•

AFTER our piss in the woods, Butras drove slowly, as if he was bored. He appeared to be deep in thought again, and sour.

"You're in a bad mood," I said to Butras. He'd been tipping his neck to make it click, a sure sign.

"Shit. Do me a favor. I'm not interested in your opinions about my moods. You're not a fucking counselor."

"See what I mean? You're angry at me, at everyone else too."

"I don't know what you're talking about," Butras said.

"I heard you're drinking again." I said it. Got personal.

He looked over at me, his eyes frozen, like my words had come from nowhere and were going nowhere.

"Don't go stupid on me, Gambell."

"You're drinking alcohol again, and you're putting me in danger doing it."

"Fuck you."

"I'm wrong?"

"Fuck you."

"Your own brother told me."

"Did he now," Butras said sarcastically. "Why don't you get out here?"

"No. I'm not getting out."

"Then don't go talking to my brother about me," he said.

"Your brother and Wilbourne both got thrown out by your father, didn't they?"

"Stay out of my business."

His words hung in the air like heat, like smoke. I rolled down my window to let the thickness escape. The night breeze had grown chilly. The streets were awash in silver-blue light. Far, far away, a bell rang.

From the time of Larry Butras' call, it had taken four hours to ask this question of my partner. Only at 10 PM did I have the nerve.

I realized that until I understood the lynching, nothing would satisfy me. Butras would say the lynching was in the past; I wanted a beginning, a middle, and an end to that story. I had suspicions, suspicions that were pure and simple about my partner and his brother and his father, and I wanted Butras to tell me they were groundless.

I remember the paleness entering his face. The stern look gave away nothing. I got the feeling there was a question he wanted to ask. He just didn't know if I was the one to ask.

Butras didn't say another word. He drove out of the woods slowly, a hard man for me to understand. I waited for an invitation to speak again or even exchange glances.

The evening's final call from dispatch came in at 11:45.

•

WHEN I joined the force, the officer with thick, silver hair who was taking my application looked at me strangely. He said, "Why would a college grad like you, in his right mind, want this job?"

A week into December, I knew that among cops the answer to the question was, "Beats working." But to the officer with the silver hair I answered, "Never wanted to do anything else. My uncle is a detective in Detroit."

I went through the list of questions they handed me. "Ever do drugs?" "Ever been arrested?" "Ever been in jail?"

When I was finished, the man with the silver hair and droopy lips asked, "Ever want to fuck up something just for the fun of it?"

I didn't understand what he was asking, but he looked me straight in the eye, a look that said: "You give me any kind of back-talking answer at all and you don't have a job."

The cop was betting that I wouldn't report him. He was betting that getting this job was important to me.

As I was walking back from the interview, I remembered a story my mother sometimes told about growing up in South Carolina before she got away to college.

"I went to an all-black school and once I was sent up to the white school to pick up something for one of my teachers. And I saw something amazing. All the tables in their cafeteria had bowls of apples on them. It was the most mysterious thing to me. I had never seen anything like it. What were bowls of apples doing on every table?"

My mother was a year past breast cancer the last time she told this story, past the surgery and the daily visits for radiation that made her sleepy and had her watching television during the day. I remember coming home riding that slow, dirty train north through New Jersey in the early evening junior year to see her most weekends. She was confident that she would get better and she did for a while.

•

AT noon on the 30th, I met Cedric for lunch in New York. A little Guatemalan place on West 59th. The decor was green and yellow like a rainforest, and it was hot. They had photographs of waterfalls. Cedric wore a Knicks T-shirt, blue and orange. We talked about how my father stayed at his job all those years, how it was comical that my father's first floor office in our home was still off limits even when I was twenty-three years old. We talked about the new job Cedric was looking for, and the end of the first month of mine.

"I hear it in your voice," Cedric said. "Getting too comfortable."

"Police work's not bad work. Maybe you should try it."

"Not my thing," he said. "People was like, ha, ha, when I told them you were a cop in your home town."

"Who?"

"Everyone."

"Who?"

"They said soon you'll have your dog, your fence, your 2.5 kids, your six uniforms in your closet, neat and pressed. I bet that town is proud to have you. At least you don't go round lynching their white folk. You're just supposed to shoot the brothers who did."

●

BEFORE I moved home, I had not spoken honestly with my father in a long time. I had always tried to hide my mistakes from him so I would not have to hear the fierce control of his voice. When I was fifteen, he betrayed me. It happened the night of July 4th, 1991.

My friend Gary and I had gone to Trygon Park to light some of the firecrackers we'd bought off of Rudy Foreman. The southwest corner of Trygon Park had a little stream running through it, nearly dry that season, and it was quiet and secluded there so we could do our business alone. Between the trees, you could make out the houses on Laurel Avenue that face the park, but most of them were dark when we got there at eight.

Gary had some M-80's and I had some smaller stuff and we set off our supply using a Bic lighter Gary had stolen from his mother's bag. It didn't take long to use up what we'd brought so we started lighting some of the dry bushes. We knew they'd burn.

We made a ring of these flaring bushes and sat in the middle and pretended we had magic skills, then we'd dash out of the circle, trying to avoid getting burned. We put out the fire with water from the stream using our hands and feet and then went to a party over at Jan Delio's.

That night, I told my mother about our setting the fires. She said she was disappointed in me and asked me to "think about my behavior and its impact on others." I didn't protest. I knew good from bad.

The next morning, there was a story in *The Record*: "Vandals Burn Up Park." It was about the fires reported by people on Laurel Avenue who had seen Trygon Park lit up in the southwest corner. Someone had called the fire department and the fire chief was quoted as saying, "Delinquents with illegal incendiary devices can cause major problems in this weather."

As I was eating breakfast with my parents, two policemen came to the back door. My father let them in, and I understood as they crossed our kitchen toward me that my mother had told him and he had called the police.

I was still sitting down when one said, "We understand you were responsible for setting fires last night in a public place."

I didn't answer. I couldn't answer.

"Come with us please," the man said. And when I stood, he guided me, with his hand on the small of my back, to their waiting car.

"I'll follow you down there," my father said.

At the police station (the new station, built two years ago, is across town from where I went that morning), one of the policeman wrote up a report and gave me a stern talk in a side room. Then he invited my father in. My father said, "The only reason that you're not going to have a permanent police record is because I asked them to fine me instead."

I later learned that I was also two months too young to carry a record into my adult years.

My father made it seem as if he were doing me a favor that day. We drove home in silence and I went to school late.

My father had not been blind to how he had humiliated me. But being the sort of man he was, and is, he believed that he was teaching me something.

I couldn't forgive him.

Dealing with my father, and my mother, forever afterward I was careful with what I admitted to.

•

THE shadow on the ground was moving like a wrestler. Pushing arms and legs across the pavement like one person trying to crawl out from underneath another who was trying to keep him down. Arms and legs working like an insect's. An invisible weight over the shadow, pressing down the small of the back as the hands tried to push the head up, and the legs tried to lift the hips.

After Butras got to the shadow, without looking to his left or right, he screamed out, "Call an ambulance."

The word GIRL came to my mind. I thought: I've shot a girl. The kid on the ground was a girl. I tried to push the thought away; I understood that there was something horrible about shooting a girl.

One minute we were driving in the car, fifteen minutes away from going home on a cold night and the next minute there was a girl on the ground in front of me, squirming and shivering convulsively.

I didn't know what I was doing when I fired.

I was not a bad cop. I had shouted a warning. I had seen a reflection, a flash.

I had shot a teenage girl who was like any one of the girls we'd passed that day.

No, it had to be a boy.

I remembered suddenly that conversation with Cedric when he said, "There's no such thing as a black John Wayne. Can you see a black John Wayne? There's no black man who's that patriotic. A black John Wayne is a maniac."

John Wayne shot a lot of people.

•

As a boy, I never liked fighting. I have strong memories of only one fight in fifth grade where I'd gotten in a few good punches but ended up with Jimmy Tuson on my chest, slapping my face around, a bunch of other guys watching, and laughing.

There were times as an adult when I wanted to fight, when I was mad enough to fight, but it hadn't happened. I had backed off figuring people are really crazy; they'd kill me for a nickel. Once, I had been trying to get on the highway, merging in from the right, and some guy in a black Ford pick-up wouldn't let me in even though the highway was empty and he could have changed lanes. So when I got on behind the pick-up I gave the asshole the finger. And the black Ford began to slow down. Down from sixty to thirty, then slower, the guy's eyes glued to his rearview mirror looking at me. The rest of the traffic was speeding past and the guy was down at fifteen miles per hour. At fifteen, it was impossible to pull out fast enough to get past him without an accident. Then the guy was signaling to the right as if to say: Let's you and me get off the highway and have more than a talk. He was going about 5 mph, virtually stopped on the interstate. Anyone who would do that was not only an asshole but crazy. As soon as the guy pulled off the road, I accelerated, never looking back.

I had felt like a coward, with a sick, nervous twisting in the back of my throat.

•

THE lights converged on the body of the boy who lay half in the light, half out of the light, light like a hole in the dark. Light that tore him apart. He was larger than I'd originally thought, half-man, half-boy. I thought of the hole in him. A hole like a leak in a tire. Small. Invisible. How could such a small hole knock you down?

I kept looking over Butras' shoulder. I wanted to see what I had done. I was alert, but in a strange, dead way.

Damaged, motionless.

If you really listen to the wind, it's uninterrupted. It must start miles away and rush when it gets near.

I had just given everything away. I had shot a boy and all I would know from that point on would be urgent and troubling.

Then I thought: when you point a gun and pull the trigger, you're a murderer. Whether you're in a uniform or not.

Then other words intervened:

Accidental . . . .

Self-defense . . . .

Anyone would have . . . .

●

IT was a Sigsauer nine millimeter with a night sight. It held eight shots and a back-up clip.

Along with the uniform and the gun, they'd also given me an asp. The asp was a metal rod that extended like a telescope when you shook out your wrist. Butras called it "nonlethal force," and he showed me how to use it like a club. I also received a cylinder of mace. Butras said they gave out the mace last because they didn't think it was important, but anyone who had been out on the street knew it was all you needed to do the job most of the time.

At the academy they told us you needed to ensure three conditions before you shot: the ability, the opportunity and fear for your life.

•

I knew I had killed a little black boy. It made me sick. It made me think of Cedric and all the times he had warned me I was going to get in trouble. It was a little black boy lying dead in that hole in the dark.

Cedric would tell me again what he had learned as a boy: if you're black there are different rules. Be careful. Figure out the rules.

I had seen the kid in the hat reach for a gun and I shot. But until Butras came back with it in his hand, I wasn't absolutely sure that it was a gun. The kid was in the dark and all I saw was a hand moving and a reflection which could have been a button. Maybe the kid was brushing something off his coat. I was surprised to see hands moving and I'm sure I screamed out, "Police, freeze."

And then I fired. I aimed and fired. I had been trained in less than a month to separate good from evil.

Even though I saw that small body fall, I did not immediately recognize what had happened, what I had done.

I thought only: I have to save my life.

●

As Butras was coming back toward me, coming back from the wall of Bryant School and the body that lay half in the shadows and half in the light, I was ready to meet him. I looked forward to seeing his face again, thankful he was with me that night. I knew we had the same purpose. But I was also alert and tense, and watching him, I was concerned that he wasn't paying attention. He wasn't protecting himself from what was out in the night, from others in that pack who would come back to see what had happened. Others who had guns aimed at us. I had to protect him.

He came at me with the swaying walk of a wrestler and I was ready to hear what he had to say. Everything Butras said seemed final and I was ready to let him help me, let him take over and things would be all right.

I was already thinking: How am I going to explain this to my father, to Cedric, to Clarise? I thought of Ethan.

It was the first time during the month that I remembered seeing Butras' breath. All the cold days we had and only then I saw the little clouds coming from his mouth, sailing off his teeth.

When he got close, I could see that his eyes were angry, but I understood. I had done something that would be with us the rest of our lives.

From ten feet away I saw that Frank Butras was not looking at me. No. In his eyes it was as if I were a phantom whom he could make vanish. It was as if he couldn't believe I was there so he made me disappear.

Butras was a small man, and his blonde hair looked almost white against the sky. His right arm looked long, as if the gun he was holding were dragging the ground.

In his left hand he had another gun. When I saw the other gun, I knew he had taken it from the boy on the ground. It was the gun I'd seen flash when the shadow had moved. The gun that had forced me to shoot.

I knew that I would be all right.

Butras' eyes were up, fierce on me. I was looking at him but also over his shoulder and around behind him, alert. He didn't seem to care about who or what was behind him. He was walking slowly. His guard was down. Whoever might be around, whatever remained out there in the night was no longer his concern. I knew this from his face because I had never seen him look so tired, so beaten.

The shots I had fired were still loud in my ears, so loud I couldn't hear myself cough. I coughed when I was nervous. Between my throat and my ears, the sound of my cough disappeared although I could feel my chest and shoulders shaking.

Butras came closer. Suddenly he was up close, flying up at my face, like we were in the center of a ring.

He said, "You stupid, fucking nigger."

I had not shot because I had simply forgotten a better way to handle things. I had not shot because I knew that some people submitted only to aggression. I had shot because I thought he was reaching into his pocket for a gun. The dispatcher had said someone had seen a gun.

Everything smelled of gunpowder.

I remembered shouting a warning: "Police."

It seems a long time ago.

•

ON the way from The Plaza to Bryant School we passed the country's largest American flag. Some people said it was just the largest flag outside of Washington, D.C. It was whipping in the wind, a good hundred feet up a pole. The flag itself must have been eight by fifteen yards. Everything around it looked off-scale. The pole itself looked like a twig. The flag was above the treetops, but if it had settled on the top branches of one of the maples, it would have covered all the leaves. It seemed out of place, a flag that size. Who made it? Why was it in the middle of Pompan?

So much else in Pompan appeared regular. It seemed to me, after I had been to every neighborhood fifteen times (seeing them now as a policeman), and inside more dining rooms and kitchens (mostly false alarms) than I cared to remember, that most of the houses in town were the same. Two or three bedrooms, automatic garage door opener, frosted glass door to the shower, stainless steel sink, garbage disposal. Houses filled with people born in Pompan. Blue collar, lower white collar, steady jobs. They were houses that were empty during the day; kids in school, parents working in New York City or out at the malls in Paramus.

The golf course was away from everything, surrounded by piney woods. The lynched man in the photograph reminded me of the fish Cedric brought back to the house, a line looped through its jaws.

•

IN the hospital's explosion of overhead lights, waiting to go to surgery, I was thinking about how Bob Esah would report the events of this night if he were still at Rutgers and was the reporter sent to cover the story, if he asked me for my side of the story.

There was no way to get it right. I heard no scream, no syllable of hurt. But there was no mistaking I'd hit him, the boy heaped on the sidewalk, half in darkness. I'd wished he had gotten up, I'd urged him to.

On TV Captain Cuvin was saying, "The teenager was hit by 3 of 8 shots fired at him beside Bryant School at about 11:50 PM. The police officers had confronted the boy after they were alerted to a report of an armed gang rampage."

Half in the light, the boy kept moving, as if he could crawl away. There was no accusation from the boy, no look of disappointment or shock or fear.

He was as silent as the lynched man.

In the explosion of lights I was thinking of how Cedric divided people. Hot and confused, I was thinking of how when I look in the mirror I see a black man. I was thinking about whether being a black man made any difference that night, whether my bringing up Butras' drinking or his brother made any difference. Then I went to sleep.

I now think of how, nine months ago, I carried a pen instead of a gun, and how I'd come to hate people I didn't know because they could do me harm, because they did do me harm. "You are the master of your own life," my father used to tell me. But it wasn't true.

I'm still raw, trying to understand the sensation. My life is not past, but most of what will happen to me probably has already happened.

The reporters will ask questions. What do other policemen do when they walk about in the night? The reporters will need an answer. They will want my unconscious motives, my psychology. They will also want evidence of my humiliation.

My father told me when he picked me at the police station he sent me to 8 years ago, "The easiest person to convict is a black man. We're already guilty. They don't even need evidence."

I will offer no answers to reporters although my mind works clearly now. I can hear the sounds for things I've already seen in my mind forty times. I pluck incident after incident from my memory now and these little explosions keep me going. I remember more and more of what I saw, and when. I listen to my pulse.

●

BUTRAS shouted, "You stupid, fucking nigger," and he held the second gun out toward me. It lay in his left palm, small and snub-nosed. It was gray and had no sheen to it and was the smallest pistol I'd ever seen,

Butras' face was furious, inhuman.

"It's a starter's pistol," Butras said. "That's all. For a race." He threw it at me. Then he approached still holding his own gun in his right hand. Close-up his breath was foul. Although I was stronger, if he had announced that he wanted to hurt me I would not have protested. Butras closed his eyes like he was resting, saving up until he felt strong enough to open them again.

Then all at once he grabbed my shirt in his hands, and he shook me. I didn't have the courage anymore to talk, to tell him to stop, and we struggled and staggered. He threw his full weight against me and we fell. Because he'd been a wrestler, both his hands went under my arms.

Maybe he meant for the gun to go off then and maybe he didn't. There is no knowing what he was thinking.

I can't work out his feelings as much as I try.

Is it possible that he has an explanation?

•

I was shot.

A surprise.

It was a close, unremarkable noise and I didn't know where it came from for a moment.

My eyes were pinched by the light, Butras bearing down on me.

When you're shot, you feel all your warmth gather in the place you've been hit. All the blood in your body moves there and the rest feels cold.

And at the same time, you feel you're invisible. You don't know the borders of your own body anymore.

Every man knows that absorbing pain, is what makes you a man. Pain meant you'd faced a challenge and even if you were scared, you couldn't pull away. You suffered.

I called on my secret courage.

And then I had pain. I would behave like a hero, I thought. On foot patrol sometimes, I plotted ways that I was going to take the pain that was sure to come. I imagined ways to escape without serious damage.

But I was too small to fight the pain. It was the desperation, laziness and horror all adding up that kept me pinned. I felt flickering movements within, but not enough to move myself. I wanted to say: that's enough pain.

My fingers locked and went stiff: Like knives.

Home, I thought. I want to rest. I was floating.

Vaguely, I was aware of how quiet it was.

Pain replaced my body.

Flat on the ground, I felt off-balance. But I didn't know why.

I thought: I have been shot.

I thought: I must keep a cool head.

I thought: I must recover.

I was rubbing my chest with a steady rhythm and my hand was getting hot. I was calming myself. I was rubbing myself in circles like I was clearing fog off a windshield. But I knew if I pressed too hard the windshield would break. I was testing my muscles to see if they worked.

It was a terrible pain.

It was a joke, man. Call off the joke.

I held my body rigid and I screamed. I pretended to myself that this scream was something important, that it would heal me.

•

WHEN it's going well, I don't notice anything during the set. I think about where I'm feeling it. I think about the pictures of the muscle groups in the anatomy book that Clarise gave me. The deep layers of the back. This is my hand, my bone, my skin. I work each muscle against the weight until it slowly and powerfully contracts. I feel huge and blood-filled. The breath's caught in me, then that weight is gone. I feel my breath and my eyes. But also a peacefulness that comes along out of my violence. I'm wide awake, tense, nerved-up. The hurt seems valuable. There are no limits, no physical limits.

I worked out on the 31st, 2:00 to 2:30 at the Y. As usual. Picked up my things, went home, got into my uniform, my shiny black shoes.

•

"THE boy's dead," my father tells me at some point, standing over my bed here, knowing I probably won't answer, thinking I can't answer, that I'm still "in shock" as the doctors have told him.

He gets close to my face. I sense his reprimand.

Noises come from my mouth unbidden.

"Dead?" I want to say in confusion. The suddenness of the shooting replaced by the suddenness of this death news.

I am startled, although he cannot tell.

My body, holding its own bullet, is now the burden of my family.

I once heard my father say to another lawyer on the phone, "Every man's got something to incriminate him. That's the way men are."

•

I had never had such pain. I couldn't bear it; it was terrible. That the pain could change, that it could get better or even disappear did not occur to me as I lay on the ground near Bryant School. If you have ever been hit as a child and remember that pain, you will understand what I was feeling. Disbelief and lack of understanding become part of the pain and added to it. And I was scared.

As you're taught when you're a child, I began to apologize. To no one in particular; to everyone. I just kept saying, "I'm sorry, I'm sorry."

When I was quiet and listened more closely than I ever had, I heard the screeches of far-off cars, the wind, a loose gate, a dog.

My blood smelled like oiled steel, like my motorcycle. The air was damp from the rains earlier.

It was too late to cry. It won't help, I thought. I was shaking with anger, anger at myself and those who hired and trained me.

A burn and a clamminess.

•

I envied Clarise's life in the city. The last night I was with her, we watched TV. Clarise had a limitless appetite for television shows about inner-city kids. Violence was what happened to them. There were those kids who could show you the scars on their legs and chests from four different shootings they had survived. There were the paralyzed victims of crossfire rolling around in their motorized chairs and typing with their teeth. There were the kids who had given it all up, who no longer were hanging with their homeboys. It was endless and pitiful and Clarise got depressed watching, but she did anyway.

"I don't know. I can't help it. It's fascinating," was all she said, when I asked her why. She was appalled by the violence that no one could escape or understand. But she was an optimist and she believed that if she watched enough she could understand it. She thought that health care would never be a success until violence was controlled.

I wanted to see basketball or a sitcom. I had no interest in shows about kids and cops.

•

ON the ground, I only wanted to sleep. I wanted to sleep on a bench in the sun on a warm day as I had done once upon a time with Clarise in the city, my head on her lap.

I could feel my wound slide open.

The feelings did not come to me in sequence, but all at once, rage, regret, a certain sort of giddiness.

I had a hole in me. I was incomplete and bleeding. Drained, like I had just finished a workout.

I wanted the weight off me, the wet weight pulling me down like the gravity I felt when I was a boy jumping off the big, split boulder in the empty lot near my elementary school, the weight of my whole body pulled into my legs, my knees filled with water.

In this world, many people have been shot.

I had just shot someone.

But now I had a hole in me from Frank Butras' bullet.

My clothes were quickly covered with blood, drenched with it. I thought of the wounds of animals and the flies crawling in.

When I was going down I thought: if people had seen me just a month before, they would have seen an ordinary black man who could disappear into a crowd of black men, no problem.

•

TERROR produced its own antidote; I was suddenly willing to die. I remembered wanting to date a white girl in high school. She was a friend, but she refused to date me, and when I asked her why, all she said was, "You know." And my mother told me when I got home, "As long as your friend thinks of you as black, you don't have a friend."

I thought of my father and his white lover.

I remembered Clarise in this tropical tank top she wore with nothing under it. When she lifted her arms and I was standing at her side, I could see in. And I could reach in.

A storm had landed on my chest. I was a breath past panic. The trees were gray, the sky was gray.

On the ground, I looked around, turning my head slowly toward my left shoulder, my right shoulder. Was anyone else there? Who was watching? Was our back-up nearby?

My mother used to tell the story of her mother visiting when we first moved to Pompan, and we were the first black family on our block. Her mother used to call us "the ocean." She said, "People will drive miles to see you, to talk at you, to throw stones at you—like the ocean."

It was Butras who shot me. The unremarkable noise had come from his gun.

I had never concentrated so hard. I knew that my survival depended on keeping my eyes open, maintaining the narrow vision of what was directly in front of me. I squinted. I obliterated everything except what I was seeing nearby and concentrated on staying alive. My face felt as if I had slipped a tight stocking over it. Something a thief might wear.

Before I went out, I heard him say, "You killed my little brother, you stupid, fucking nigger. That's my brother on the ground."

•

THE moment before I fired, the moment the boy's face emerged from the shadow and he lifted his arm, I knew it was Butras' brother. I have a hard time making these events obey anything but the logic of nightmare, but now I know that before I shot, I saw it was Larry Butras, and he was turning, or reaching and there was a flash, and that I hit him below the right shoulder blade.

This is how I spend my days, having second thoughts about the irrecoverable. Trying to explain it all to myself before I speak, before words. It will be impossible to say anything that matters.

Did I believe he'd done the lynching, and that's why I fired? Because I believed he'd gotten away with it, protected as a member of Butras' family by men in the station who were simply doing justice for their city, who didn't want Clarence Wilbourne around either? Did I fire because of the likeness, brother to brother? Like so much else, this is only a theory, a version of myself as avenger.

If Butras had wanted to kill me, he could have as I lay on the frozen ground after his first shot. Does my living presence in this bed mean his firing was an accident?

Perhaps I returned to Pompan searching for death. Why else had I come back? Why else was I a policeman?

In the station in December, there was always a level of meaning I was hopeless to interpret. I listened to know what topics not to bring up. When I saw that no one in that station wanted to talk about the lynching, why didn't I quit asking?

The anger in me is gone; I am only afraid.

I saw Captain Cuvin at the news conference on New Year's Day:

] 192 [

"Donald Gambell did what he was trained to do. He reacted to a situation in the way he was taught to react. If it had been me I would have done the same thing."

But would he have?

I know nothing about Frank Butras' whereabouts tonight although we spent the last month of nights together.

In the dull heat of this mechanical bed, in this white room, I wait for the nurse to return. Where does pain go when it goes away?